Teddy and the
Darkgate

Simon M Garrett

grŵpgwyn

From the back cover:

"Nobody takes a teddy seriously — and that might just save Teddy's life.

"Not that he'll notice; Teddy is too focused on reaching the lady of his dreams, avoiding a vomiting baby and finding a way to get from Aberystwyth to Clehonger, despite being unable to read a map.

"Behind the scenes, things are moving. Dark things. Dark things that would happily kill an idealistic Teddy who's bumbling through the big, wide world. But the biggest threat is to Teddy's dreams. Will a world of cynical animals and indifferent humans drain him of his hopes and wide-eyed trust, or will he find a way to escape danger while holding on to his naive belief that he can do something amazing?

"And what *does* it all have to do with The Darkgate?"

First published in Great Britain in 2011
grŵpgwyn "The Forge", HR2 8BU

Copyright © 2014 Simon M. Garrett
"Teddy" names, characters and related indicia are copyright grŵpgwyn 2014.

Simon M. Garrett has asserted his moral rights
A CIP record of this book is available from the British Library

ISBN 978-0-9569246-3-6

Fourth Edition

http://www.grwpgwyn.com/books/teddy-and-the-darkgate

For Bertie, Oliver and Joanne.

Preface

When all this began, Teddy lived a few miles outside Aberystwyth, in a slate-grey, wet-stone cottage with Joanne and me. I'll be up-front: Teddy is a teddy. Now, this may sound obvious, but it's something you'll come to understand is important to him. And since it was his idea to write this book, he wanted it right here, up front. And also, rather obviously, he's a Live toy.

Teddy would have written this book himself, but just about the only writing tool he's mastered is the crayon (he says he would use a big red one), and not too many agents or publishers are keen on reading manuscripts written in red crayon, with three words on each page. So, although Teddy can read and write fairly well (unlike most teddies) I've nevertheless written it all down for him on my computer, which is probably more sensible.

Teddy 'belongs' to me, and I care for him, which matters because it keeps him Alive and Awake (both with capital-As). Usually, it takes a *lot* of love to Wake a live toy, but some teddies start Waking the moment someone hugs them and gives them even a hint of affection. Teddy remembers being hugged by a little girl, while he was still in a bin of teddies in the toy section of the vast shop that was selling him. The girl loved Teddy but her mum wouldn't buy him for her; nevertheless, it Woke him enough for him to look around for a few minutes.

Another teddy was vaguely Awake, and he mumbled how he had been hugged by one of the factory girls who'd made them in Vietnam. Apparently, the factory was hot and noisy but not especially interesting, not to a teddy at least. However, for a teddy to have known his maker is remarkable. The factory girl had needed to get back to work and put him back on the conveyor belt, and he soon fell Asleep because, if a teddy isn't hugged, it will eventually go back to Sleep until someone loves it again.

But none of this explains why a grown man like me owns a two-foot teddy bear — I bought Teddy because I was struggling with the idea of becoming a father. I thought, "Let's see what happens if I have to 'look after' this big teddy," in the same way American school children have to carry around a bag of flour for a week and pretend it's a baby, so they'll realise that having a baby is a big responsibility. Well, I already knew it was a huge, *massive* responsibility to father a child, but I bought Teddy to help convince myself that maybe I could do it anyway. Then Teddy Woke up. It was a bit of a shock, but you hear about these things and initial any concerns turned out to be misplaced: Teddy has a charm that disarms you of any worries, and soon everyone was happy about the way things were working out. So I thought having a baby might be a good idea.

Now, apparently, some teddies are quiet and say very little, and some are like Teddy. He talks *a lot*. Also, he has his own way of speaking which is a little unusual. You or I might say, "I'm going to get a glass of orange juice," but Teddy would say something like, "I ffink, I would like some orangey joosey Simon, please, actchully." I would remind Teddy that teddies don't need to drink anything, but Teddy still likes to try anyway. (The most surprising thing is that he *can* drink, and it doesn't end up leaking out of him, but that's another matter for another time.) Of course, when he does drink orange juice, his snout gets all sticky and has to be cleaned up, which he *hates*. Sometimes the only thing that will stop him from scoffing pawfuls of strawberry jam sponge cake is the threat of being put into the washing machine. Joanne used to suggest this casually, and Teddy would panic until he realised she was joking.

Anyway, the point is that Teddy likes to talk (as apparently I do), so I got him to talk about all of his travels, and I've written them down as he recounted them. (That's why it says, "Simon" did this and said that in the text, rather than "I", because it's from Teddy's point of view). I've also added some details that Teddy forgot, and some things that Teddy didn't realise were happening until we tried to write them down, and occasionally Joanne added some thoughts too.

- Chapter 1 -

Teddy And The Baby

For the past hour, a stripe of golden sunlight had been tracking across the darkened bedroom, let in through a crack in the curtains. Its warmth finally reached Teddy's leg paws, which poked out over the edge of his sleeping-chair; he woke, stretched, yawned. This, Teddy decided, was a wonderful way to wake up.

Squinting at the brightness between the curtains; it was just possible for Teddy to make out the world beyond, at the beginning of a particularly sunny late autumn day. When he looked down at his leg paws again, he had to wait for his eyes to re-adjust to the darkness of the room before he could see his surroundings, all the while keeping his paws still in the sun's glow. Then he wiggled his legs up and down madly for a few seconds and watched the sun dance on his fur. Teddy was content. He closed his eyes, relaxed and allowed time to flow, feeling its slow pace. He had a fuzzy little thought in his head, and the thought that he realised he was having was that today, like many other days, it was good to be a teddy.

Simon and Joanne, in the bed next to Teddy, had not yet woken. Simon, who was nearest, was making relaxed rhythmic breathing sounds; Joanne was lying on her side, facing the other way, and Teddy couldn't hear anything much from her. She was slightly silhouetted and her shape rose and fell with her near-silent breathing. Then she made a sharp little squeak and rolled over. Her forehead wrinkled in discomfort. Then it passed, she relaxed and resumed her quiet breathing.

Teddy didn't understand, but she seemed fine now, so he closed his eyes. "Mmm. Der warm happy," he thought to himself, and he drifted back to sleep.

::

Teddy woke again, and somewhat slowly reasoned that it must have been quite a lot later because the bed was empty. "Hm. I wunder where dey arr?" he thought. "Huh! I'm der funny heavy-sleeper teddy!" He laughed a roly-poly little laugh. Teddy is amused by a lot of things that most people probably wouldn't find funny at all. He glanced down from his chair: it was quite a way to the floor, but it was okay, he did this every day. He wiggled forwards on his bottom so his legs dangled completely off the edge of the chair, then turned around onto his tummy, and lowered himself off the edge. Soon he was hanging on only by his arm paws, and then he let himself drop. "Bonk!" he said out loud, and chortled to himself, as he padded over the carpet towards the door.

"Hm... I fiiink I want a drinkie," he thought, so he crossed the landing and bustled into the bathroom. There was the toilet, all white, and inviting, and full of water. Simon and Joanne had told him many times that drinking out of the toilet was a very unpleasant thing to do (because he'd spread germs everywhere) and a pointless thing to do (because teddies don't need to drink) but Teddy wanted to do it anyway; it was as much about the challenge as anything else. He put his paws on the toilet seat, pulled himself up, and stuck his head down the toilet bowl to slurp, water splashing everywhere. When he finished he levered himself out of the bowl, and dropped onto the floor, "Mmmm. Dat's better!"

At that moment, Teddy heard the backdoor slam.

"Uh-oh! Day're back, and I got der wet paws! Oh no!"

He ran out of the bathroom as fast as his paws could carry him, then he slipped to a stop because he'd gone the wrong way. He turned around and ran back past the bathroom towards the bedroom, as Joanne put her foot on the bottom step of the stairs. He searched around the bedroom for something, anything, to dry his paws and snout on, but only found a pair of Simon's trousers.

Joanne and Simon clumped up the stairs as Teddy grabbed the trousers and dried himself with a few quick scrubs. He climbed onto his sleeping-chair as fast as he could and pretended to be asleep, just as they entered the room.

"Teddy," said Simon. "Joanne's got some news."

"I'm asleep!" said Teddy nervously.

"No, you're not, Teddy; you're talking to me so you're aw— What happened to my trousers?!"

"Nuffing! Nuffing! It wasn't me!" lied Teddy.

"Simon," interrupted Joanne, "we've got something to say."

"Hm, yes."

"Teddy," said Joanne, "I'm pregnant."

There was a pause as Teddy rolled the news over in his head.

"Dat's ... good, isn't it?" said Teddy, with a quizzical look. His head tilting to one side as he tried to grasp the implications.

"Well, we think so. Though we are bit nervous to be honest."

"Why?"

"Because we've never had to look after a baby before."

"Why?"

"Because we've never been parents before."

"Why?"

"BECAUSE I'VE NEVER BEEN PREG—"

"You know," said Simon. "We've already got some experience with little ones."

::

Months went by, winter and spring came and went, and all the while Joanne's tummy bump grew bigger and bigger. Teddy was confused. Simon kept saying that there was a baby inside Joanne, but that was just silly because surely a baby would never be happy *inside* someone! Nevertheless, Teddy did understand that a baby was soon going to come to live with them. He couldn't quite put his paw on the reason why, but it bothered him.

In early summer the day finally came. Teddy woke to the

sound of painful groaning. Simon and Joanne were both awake, and Joanne looked very uncomfortable and was the one making the noises. Teddy wasn't properly awake, and didn't say anything, but he saw them leave. Eventually, he worked out that this meant they were probably going to get the baby from the 'hospital' that Joanne had mentioned. It sounded a bit like a shop that gave you a baby; he hoped they had enough money.

He waited all day, amusing himself around the house, and when it began to get dark he slept fitfully. A couple of times he awoke with a jolt and waited nervously in the dark until he fell asleep again.

Some hours later, Simon returned looking exhausted, without Joanne.

"Is Joanne okay, Simon?"

"Yeah" said Simon, with heavy, dozy eyes. "She's fine; I don't know how she did it. She was amazing. The baby was born just after one o'clock this morning. I stayed with them a while, then they needed to get their sleep and the nurses shooed me away. Really tired now."

Simon was mumbling, and Teddy had to listen hard to understand him. "Hope they're fast asleep," Simon yawned. "Baby was a bit noisy."

"So you had enough monies den?"

"Huh?"

"For der baby?"

"Um. You don't need money to get a baby. It ..." Simon yawned again, "Hm, I'll explain in the morning. I *really* need to get some sleep now. You'll see the baby in a few days. We've called him 'Bertie'." Simon's words trailed off again.

"Okay, dat's really good ..." Teddy also yawned a big yawn, happy now he knew that Simon and Joanne were fine. "I tired too, night-night." But Simon was already asleep, almost face-down on the bed, in his clothes.

::

A few days later, Joanne was strong enough to return from the hospital. Teddy wasn't sure why she was so tired, after all that lying-down-in-a-bed that she'd been doing. He soon found out. The baby had a scream that was louder than the smoke alarm. Nobody slept well. Baby screamed in the night, and he screamed in the day. He'd scream for a feed, then he'd bring it all back up again and scream some more. He'd scream when he was lonely, and when there were too many people around him. Sometimes, he'd scream for no apparent reason, without stopping. Teddy missed the quiet, he wanted things they way they had been. Once, baby had sucked on Teddy's nose and covered it with mucus. Simon and Joanne smiled tired smiles and wiped it off, but Teddy wasn't so amused.

The first few days of baby being at home were hard on everyone; even baby: it turned out that baby Bertie had a fairly common problem with his kidneys. A few months later all would be well, but for now he was in some pain, and that was why he screamed so much.

::

After five days of housebound sleep deprivation, Joanne and Simon had no choice but to drive to town to buy food. They were exhausted, and it seemed like a massive undertaking, so they tried to think of a way to make it easier.

"Do you think Bertie would like Teddy to sit next to him in the back of the car?" asked Joanne.

"Yes, yes, it might help to calm him," Simon agreed.

So, today was the day that Joanne and Simon were going to take Teddy in the car again. Teddy had been in the car before, but that was a while ago. Long enough ago that Joanne and Simon thought that maybe last time hadn't been so bad after all. It's also possible the lack of sleep had addled their brains.

The only other time Teddy had been in the car, he'd waved at almost every car and person that he saw for over an hour. Teddies don't normally do that. It caused cars to swerve. An old lady had walked into a lamp post. People almost never see teddies waving at them. In what little thought Simon gave to the matter, he hoped that — since Teddy was sitting next to a baby — people would probably convince themselves that it must have been the baby that had moved. To be fair, that part would work out fairly well. So, they got ready to go to town.

It took them 47 minutes to get ready. First the baby needed changing; then they had to tick off, one-by-one, all the things that baby needed to go with him (that's nappies, bottom wipes, bags for waste wipes and nappies, nappy cream, clothes, and a tiny coat, just in case); then they put baby in his car cot, which was a ridiculously complex exercise in itself, with multiple straps and impossible clips everywhere, and baby's belongings were stowed in the boot.

When they'd finally put everything in the car, where Teddy had been waiting for almost the whole time, they heard a *sound*. It was the unmistakable sound of a baby filling its nappy with wet solids from its bottom. So, baby needed to be carried into the house and changed again, which took ages because neither Simon nor Joanne were very good at it. To be honest, they were so bad, that they got baby poo all over Bertie's clothes and they had to completely change what he was wearing, which made him scream. Then baby needed to be cuddled, and calmed down, and loved, and only then could they try putting him back in the car.

So it took 47 minutes, but they had all made it to the car, and they set off to town for their first trip with Bertie. Teddy wasn't happy. Simon and Joanne had hardly noticed him and he'd been sitting in the car all that time. On the way, all they talked about was the baby, and all the baby did was sleep and then scream and poo again (as they entered the supermarket car park), and it dribbled. Teddy looked on in horrified awe.

Simon asked Teddy if he'd like to have baby on his lap.

"Errr, no ffank you. Not really," said Teddy. "He's got a smelly bottom again."

"Oh, go on, here he is," grinned Simon, supporting Bertie's floppy little head as he placed him on Teddy's lap so Bertie could look at Teddy.

"See," smiled Simon, "he likes you!"

Unfortunately, it was at exactly this point that baby vomited milk all over Teddy's face and chest.

"ARRRRRGGGHHH! DER BABY 'SPLODED!" screamed Teddy, "ALL OVER ME!"

"Simon!" clipped Joanne, in a voice that could etch glass, "What are you DOING?"

"Oh! Oh! Oh!" flapped Simon, ineffectually.

Joanne came round the car and gave Simon some wipes so he could clean Bertie, top and bottom, then gently pushed the new father and baby out of the way and started to clean Teddy.

"I don't like it! I don't like it!" panicked Teddy. "I liked ffings dey way day were before der baby!"

"Oh come on Teddy, you'll be fine in a minute."

But he wasn't. In a minute, Teddy was still being cleaned up. In an hour, he was still wet. The next day, and every day for at least a week, he stank of gone-off, milky, baby sick, so nobody wanted to cuddle him, not that they had had the time anyway. And Teddy was definitely not fine. He wasn't coping at all. Every time baby came near him, it seemed Teddy got covered in slime or sick. Once, while the baby was being changed, he managed to spray Teddy with wee on Teddy's arm. Teddy ran around in circles, shaking his arm, appalled and alarmed.

By now, Teddy felt almost continuously ignored, and he was beginning to realise that it was going to carry on like this for a long time. Teddy felt bad, because he knew that teddies usually enjoy being with babies and children, but how could anyone enjoy this? He wanted things to be as they had been before. He didn't want things to have changed even one little bit.

Then something happened: an awakening event. A day that changed Teddy forever.

It began with a farmer. He drove by Teddy's house in his tractor, and put-putted away and around the corner. He only stopped for a few seconds to open a gate, so he could drive though and fix out the field's fences ready for winter. But it was too long. There was a smashing sound that had Teddy, Joanne and Simon all rushing to the lounge window at the same time. A tourist, who was driving too fast, hadn't stopped and had crashed into the farmer's trailer. The car deflected sideways off the trailer, turned over lazily, and scraped up the road on its roof blocking the traffic on the other side. Luckily, no one was badly hurt, but the road was blocked in both directions, and soon the cars were backed up outside Teddy's house.

Simon rushed out to offer help, while Teddy watched from an upstairs window. People were fidgeting in their cars and music played from their open windows. It was a steaming hot summer's day and it stoked their annoyance. Simon talked to the farmer and the tourist while, back in the house, an exhausted Joanne retuned to lie down on the bed while Bertie slept for a few minutes. Teddy stared at the crash site, a couple of hundred metres away, through the window. Simon, the farmer, and the tourist were still talking, animatedly, but too far away for Teddy to hear what they were saying.

Then Teddy noticed … her. She was in a car slightly to the left of his vantage point, lying on the back shelf of a 4x4, looking up at the sky. She was the most gorgeous lady teddy he had ever seen, with beautiful, perfect white fur that had been brushed in exactly the same direction. She almost shone with elegance and appeal. Two seconds later, Teddy was in love. Without a doubt, she was a teddy to adore.

Lady Teddy appeared a bit bored and she was looking slowly up at the sky and all around. "Look at ME!" thought Teddy, but she didn't. She glanced left at the trees on Teddy's side of the valley. She looked up at the birds overhead. She studied her paws. She looked up at the chimney pot of Teddy's house. She looked at Teddy. She looked RIGHT AT TEDDY. Teddy's stuffing flooded with excitement. He waved, madly.

To his amazement, she smiled at him, and to Teddy's even greater delight, she made a flirty shape with her snout, a bit like an air-kiss, and then she winked at him. At that moment, two small human hands grabbed her legs and pulled her towards the back seat and out of view.

"NOOOO!" said Teddy, out loud. He was bursting to see her beautiful face again. Teddy jumped off the window ledge so fast that he bounced like a ball when he landed on the floor and had to scramble onto his feet. He raced downstairs and into the lounge to get to the front door. Although he reached it quickly, however hard he tried, his paws slipped on the brass of the door knob and he couldn't get it to turn. So, he quickly poddled over to the lounge window and scrambled up, just in case he could catch another glimpse of Lady Teddy through the side windows of her car.

To his horror, he saw that Simon and the farmer had managed to get the tractor to limp out of the way, and now the traffic was moving. In a less than a minute, Lady Teddy's car would be on its way. Teddy scanned the car for anything he might remember, anything to help him find her again. All he saw were some words on a sticker on the back window. He was not the world's fastest reader, so it took him a few seconds, but the words definitely said 'Clehonger Cars.' He remembered the words. He held on to them in his head. She was the beautiful, wonderful, gorgeous Lady Teddy of Clehonger Cars, he loved her, and he would find her one day.

After that day, life in the house seemed worse. All Teddy wanted was for Lady Teddy to come to see him, and for the baby to go back to the hospital shop. He wanted to wake up warm, in the sun, quiet and happy and loved.

Reality was different, however. He was miserable. It was not just because he spent most of his time dwelling on the way they used to be, and wanting to be with Lady Teddy, but also because he hardly ever saw Simon or Joanne properly and was lonely.

When he did see Simon, Teddy told him about Lady Teddy, and Simon had helped him look up Clehonger on the map on his computer. Apparently, it was a small place near Hereford, in England, just over the border from Wales. Then the baby had needed to be changed, and Simon had had to leave before they'd finished their chat.

Teddy sat in his upstairs window, looking up at the sky and hoping to see Lady Teddy's car. He spent hours each day sitting in the window, hoping for her. Two red kites flew through the air above the Welsh cottage, looking for carrion to eat below them. They hovered like enormous leaves on a warm breeze. Teddy ever so slightly held his arms out a bit further as he watched them elegantly circle with their soft, still wings, far above him. They were free, in the sky.

"Teddy, can you come here a moment please?" called Simon.

"Coming," said Teddy, and he plodded glumly towards the baby room, where he heard Simon changing Bertie.

"Can you pass me the baby wipes please?" asked Simon as he held baby Bertie's bottom clear of the changing mat with one hand, and folded up a dirty nappy in the other. The nappy was dropped into a washing bin.

Teddy passed the wipes to Simon. He tried to be enthusiastic, but when he saw baby Bertie he felt a little bit angry. As he noticed his anger, the cold, dank feeling spread into Teddy's stuffing again. "I'm supposed to love babies, I ffink? Isn't dat what teddies are for?" he thought to himself.

Simon gently lifted baby Bertie a little higher by his legs to wipe his bottom, and at that moment the baby fired a stream of yellow poo in an arch up into the air, then down over the changing table, onto his baby clothes next to the table, and on to the nursery carpet right next to Teddy.

"Eeee!" squealed Teddy, running quickly out of the room.

"Sorry Teddy!" Simon shouted after him, somewhat absentmindedly, because he now had to work out how to finish changing baby Bertie without getting any of the poo (that was everywhere) on anything else.

Teddy didn't notice; he was disgusted and dismayed. It was all too much. He didn't like the biting and the mucus and the grabbing, and he hated the wee and the sick that needed to be wiped out of his fur, but he could only imagine how long it would take to get the smell of baby poo out of his fur. Teddy padded out of the room and sat in his window on the top corridor. He couldn't take this any longer. No one seemed to care about him, and he couldn't stop thinking about Lady Teddy and her beautiful fur, and being hugged by her.

Workmen were repairing the road where it had been damaged by the tourist's car and there was a row of cars waiting to be directed around the road works, by a bored looking workman holding a Stop/Go lollipop.

Then it came to him. An idea so simple, and so exciting that he said, "Oooh!" out loud. He would, right now, try to *find* Lady Teddy. Lady Teddy of Clehonger. The destination 'Clehonger' would surely be enough. When he found the town, he would simply ask the first person he saw where Lady Teddy lived, and they would tell him. It was a brilliant plan. It was foolproof.

Without further thought, Teddy bumped downstairs on his bottom, ran into the lounge, climbed up onto the arm of an armchair, and leapt onto the lounge windowsill. The window was wide open; all he had to do was jump. He paused for a second to look around the lounge one last time. Then he jumped out of the window, landed in the front yard and waited behind the low wall of the front yard for a car to stop.

However, the thing that stopped in front of Teddy's house wasn't a car, it was a motorbike and sidecar. This was *better* than a car, it was absolutely ideal for Teddy. It stopped and its rider watched the red kites flying overhead. Teddy ran for the sidecar, scrambled in and pulled the awning over himself. He hardly dared breathe in case the rider had seen or heard, but the rider had been far too busy looking at the birds of prey swooping through the sky above, and the motorbike was far too noisy for him to hear anything.

The lollipop man got the signal on his walkie-talkie from his mate at the other end of the road works. He turned his lollipop to 'Go', and the motorbike sidecar, rider and Teddy revved off and disappeared around the corner. Teddy was gone.

- Chapter 2 -

Teddy And The Crocodiles Under The Bridge

The motorbike was violently noisy, and it seemed to Teddy to be moving faster than anything on earth; this was partly because the sidecar in which he was sitting was travelling no more than thirty centimetres above the ground, and partly because the motorbike rider was breaking the speed limit with spectacular abandon.

From Teddy's vantage point, peeking from under the sidecar's awning, hedges and road markings were blurred; trees came and went in a blink, and even the hills and valleys glided past at a surprising rate. It was a lot for a teddy to take in, and all the time, it was insanely noisy, the motorbike engine beating itself hard to maintain the speed required by its master.

Teddy had never really seen the countryside like this before. He'd always had the same old view from the upstairs window at home, or a couple of times seen it sedately from a car, but now the air rushed past his snout and invaded his fur.

Roads and lanes twisted, higgledy-piggledy, across rounded hills, and almost all of them were flanked by hedges, green with their summer leaves. Houses and farms were scattered upon the hills, usually standing alone, but occasionally side-by-side. Sometimes, a single tree might punctuate a bare, rocky hill but, more often, they grew in forestry copses or woods, or right up to the roadside hedges.

Teddy found looking at distant hills made him feel less sick than the blur of green and brown and grey that was next to his sidecar.

It wasn't long before they reached a small village and the motorbike slowed to a more sensible pace.

Now the houses were grouped together into lanes and streets. These were houses that he'd never seen before and Teddy found himself wondering if he'd ever see them again. Could this really be a one-way trip? He remembered Lady Teddy and knew there was no need to think like that, all he wanted was to be loved by her and her family, then everything would be perfect.

The motorbike left the village, turned to the right round a roundabout, and they accelerated hard; soon everything was blurring again. It was a lot for a teddy to handle, and he hoped it wasn't too far to Clehonger. Maybe he could walk? He wasn't sure since he hadn't brought a map, but that was because he couldn't read a map. Maybe he needed some help? He chortled to himself: no, he'd be fine.

A few minutes later the motorbike slowed down again and then crossed the road to park in a lay-by on the right, under some trees. The motorbike man dismounted and walked briskly towards the wood. He glanced left and right and quickly stepped over the low fence, into the trees, to relieve himself.

Teddy thought. Travelling like this wasn't much fun, and he wasn't sure that the man was going near Clehonger. Perhaps he was going the wrong way? He changed his mind, he *did* need some help; he'd have to find someone he could trust, and he didn't trust this lunatic motorbike man. Making sure the man didn't see him, Teddy lifted the awning and wriggled out of the sidecar onto the ground. SPLASH! Right into a puddle.

"Bovver-bottoms!" swore Teddy, looking down to see his leg paws totally under water — but there was no time to waste, he splashed out of the puddle and ran off, away from the motorbike, toward a bridge.

As he got closer to the bridge, he noticed two things. Firstly, it was a road bridge over a small river, which Teddy thought was quite exciting because he'd never seen a bridge up-close before, or a river. Secondly, there were faint snapping sounds coming from under the bridge.

Teddy glanced over his shoulder to make sure the sounds weren't being made by the man walking on sticks and twigs, on his way back to the motorbike ... they weren't; the sounds were coming from under the bridge. Teddy was intrigued. What could make a noise like that? He waddled closer to the bridge. Definite snapping sounds, and with the snapping the sounds of whispering coming from the darkness.

"Shh!"

>SNAP<

"Someone there ..."

>SNIP-SNAP<

" ... don't let them hear us yet ..."

>SNIP-SNAP-SNIP<

" ... ooh, they're coming!"

>SNAP<

>SNIP-SNAP<

There were several of them, and whoever it was had just stopped talking.

VROOOOOM! Teddy jumped in surprise as the motorbike roared into life behind him. He glanced over, but the man wasn't looking at him, he was looking at the road to make sure no one was coming. The road was clear, and the man roared away, disappearing in seconds, and Teddy was alone.

>SNAP<

Apart from whoever was under the bridge.

Being a trusting kind of teddy, Teddy wanted to go down to

the river to say hello, so he worked his way down the bank, toward the bridge.

"Hello? It's me!" said Teddy.

>SNAP<

"Hello," said a thin, sneery voice. "Why don't you come closer so we can see you?"

"Oh! Okay den!" said Teddy, happy to have made some new friends out here in the big, wide world.

He poddled down the river bank and began to make out shapes in the gloomy darkness under the bridge. The shapes were moving in the water, and appeared to be green. Very dark green, and wet, and shiny.

"We're here!" said another equally thin, almost mocking voice. "Come a little closer, we want to see you."

"Here I am!" giggled Teddy, happy that his new friends wanted to meet him. His paws pushed aside the untidy grass around his tummy until he came out under the bridge, in the darkness in which they lived.

"Would you like to come and play a game? We absolutely love playing games," they added, sickeningly truthfully.

"Huh?" said Teddy, entirely clueless about what game his friends under the bridge might play with him.

"We're very good at our game you know."

"Oh," said Teddy, still mystified, "Um, who are you?"

"Can't you see us?" replied a voice.

"It a bit dark, actchully," said Teddy.

"We are crocodiles. Who are you? What's your name, ffffff-fella?" smarmed the crocodile, with a glint in the darkness.

Teddy began to feel uneasy. Something told him not to tell the crocodile who he was.

"Oh, I'm T— um, I'm definitely *not* Teddy."

"Oh. That's odd because you look like a 'teddy'," squirmed the croc, pretending to believe Teddy.

"Well, um, I'm not! I'm, um, I'm, um, 'Mr Octopus'. Dat's me!" And he waggled his arms around as if to prove his point.

"Okay, nice to meeeet you, Mr Octopus." The croc was really enjoying playing with its prey.

"Huh?" said Teddy looking around, "Oh, Octopus! Me! Ha har! Dat's me!"

Something, and he still wasn't sure what it was, was telling Teddy he had to escape right now. Unfortunately, the crocs sensed it too, and they began to float slowly towards Teddy.

Teddy backed away from the darkness, up into the thick grass of the river bank.

"Oh no you don't!" laughed the lead croc, confidently, and he quickened his pace, thrashing and splashing his tough tail in the water to gain enough forward momentum to mount the bank.

Teddy panicked and fell backwards.

"Arrrgghh!" he cried.

"Yes, that's right!" said the croc, two others now flanking him, completely out of the water and striding toward him.

Teddy turned over and scrambled up the bank with all four paws, but the crocs were gaining on him, and joined him out in the light. Teddy's paws slipped on the mud and grass, but eventually he gained traction and crawled up the bank; however, the lead croc was getting dangerously close, almost close enough to try snapping at Teddy.

A car drove into view on the road and the crocs immediately froze, then sank down into the grass, so as not to be seen. Teddy had no such concerns and carried on running.

In the car, a small boy was rather surprised to see a teddy sprinting, as if for his life. The boy opened his mouth in amazement and waved slowly; Teddy waved back, albeit with a grim look on his face. The car crossed the bridge and the crocs sprang up and redoubled their efforts to catch Teddy.

Teddy glanced over his shoulder and saw them gaining on him

again. What was he going to do? There was no way he could outrun them, and there was nowhere to go to escape them. He thought about climbing a tree, but he'd never climbed a tree before, and didn't know how to do it.

Luckily for Teddy, a Landrover Defender came around the corner, pulling a trailer. Again the crocs stopped moving and sank down into the long grass. The Landrover pulled into the lay-by and stopped with a squeak of its brakes and a jolt. The farmer, who was driving the Landrover, immediately leaned across to the passenger side and disappeared below the level of the window, presumably to get something out of a glove compartment or off the floor. This was Teddy's only chance. He ran, like he'd never run before and half-jumped, half-scrambled into the trailer.

The crocs snapped in anger from their hiding place and the farmer sat up quickly and looked around with a puzzled expression at the noise he thought he'd just heard. However, he had retrieved whatever it was that he needed, so he checked his mirrors while the Landrover began to roll over the stones and up to the edge of the road. The farmer checked left and right. Nothing was coming so he drove off, over the bridge, unaware that he was leaving behind some very annoyed crocodiles.

Teddy was elated. He'd escaped! He hadn't been ripped to shreds! He was still alive.

"Grrrrrrrrrr!" growled whoever was in the trailer with him.

- Chapter 3 -

Teddy And The Forlorn Howl

"Please don't eat me! Please don't eat me!" pleaded Teddy to the black and white dog in the trailer with him.

"Hm. Well, you're certainly squeaky enough to be food, but no, I'm not going to eat you, not least because it looks like I'd be spitting fluff out of my mouth for days," said the dog, dryly. "I'm just waiting for your *very good* explanation for why you are in my master's trailer."

"I was being chased by der crocodiles!" said Teddy, honestly.

"You were being 'chased by der crocodiles'," said the dog slowly, ending with a sigh of disbelief.

"Yes," said Teddy, "Day wanted to eat me!"

"You think *I'm* going to eat you. You think the '*crocodiles*' were going to eat you. Do you think *every*one wants to eat you?" asked the dog, shaking his head. "I spend my days herding sheep: I see a lot, and I'm very good at my job, and I'm not stupid. I travel up and down this road many times every single week. There are no crocodiles, here or anywhere else."

"Dare are, dare are!" said Teddy, still out of breath, pointing back towards the bridge.

"Back there?" said the black and white dog, without even a hint of amusement, and absolutely no expectation of a sane answer.

"Yes, under der bridge back dare. They seemed to be friendly, and den day tried to eat me!"

"Well, I'm sure crocodiles are like that," said the black and white dog, rolling his eyes. The dog waited for Teddy's reply.

"I don't fink you believe me," realised Teddy, at last.

"Really? How careless of me to let it show," said the dog, ironically. He sighed: "What were you *doing* there in the first place?"

"Um, well, I saw a Lady Teddy, after the baby was sick on me — he has der yukky nose goo too — and I want to hug der Lady Teddy, so I ran out of der house and got in der moto-bikey-pod-ffingy, and den I didn't know how to get to der Lady Teddy, so I got out of der pod and den the crocodiles happened! And den I escaped into dis trailer, and den you went 'grrrr'."

The sheepdog was as motionless as a dog can be when sitting in a moving trailer. He blinked as the trailer rattled over a pothole, jolting them both, plus the bags of sheep feed and fencing materials that were in the trailer with them both.

"You're a strange little creature, aren't you?" said the dog.

"No, not really, no! Its der trooff!"

Realising the conversation could continue in this vein for a while, the dog simply gave up: "Look, I'm Gruff, I'm a sheep dog. Clearly you're *mad*, but it's surprisingly nice to meet you anyway."

"Nice to meet you too, Gruff."

"There we go. Some sanity at last!"

Gruff's mouth opened into a happy dog-grin, and neither teddy nor dog said a word. They simply felt the wind in their fur and the gentle jolting of the trailer as it trundled along at a sensible speed.

"Um, where are we going?" asked Teddy.

"Llandegley," said Gruff. Teddy was none the wiser, having no idea even where his old home had been, but he knew he needed to find a way to Lady Teddy.

"Is dat near to Clehonger?"

"Lle hon beth?" said Gruff.

"Huh?"

"Ah, I thought you were speaking Welsh. If that's a place then I've never heard of it."

"Dat's right, it is, but I don't know how to get there."

"Ah, well, you'll need a map. You'll need a human to read it. Or a hedgehog."

"A hedgehog?"

"Yes, they can read anything. They spend all their spare time curled up with a few leaves! HAHAHAHA!"

Teddy's brow became furrowed.

"It was a joke," added Gruff. "You didn't get it, but that's okay; it wasn't a very good joke anyway."

"So we need a human?"

"I'm not sure 'we' is the right word, but I'll help you if I can. I've got work to do when I get to Llandegley; we're picking up some sheep to take back to Llanguirig, my master and me."

"You have a master?"

"Of course, don't you?" said Gruff half-surprised, and half disapproving that Teddy might not.

"Er, no. I don't ffink so. Not any more for sure. Only me now!"

"No master? Okay. Hm. No master? So what do you do every day? Who looks after you?"

"Um. I'm trying to find Lady Teddy; dare's no one else at der moment, only me."

Teddy was beginning to feel cold and worried in his tummy.

"Well, that's, um, unusual," said Gruff. "Never heard of anyone without a master before. And trying to do stuff on your own as well. Hm." It was clear he didn't approve at all.

Teddy couldn't work out why Gruff was against the idea of someone 'on their own', without a master, but being a happy sort of teddy, he assumed he'd misunderstood.

"I'm hoping that Lady Teddy's family will look after me."

"Ah, you're *looking* for a master. Well, like I said, it sounds like you need to get help from a human. It's not easy though, because they can't understand us."

"Day can understand *me* doh."

"They *can?*" said Gruff, somewhat impressed.

"Um, yeah."

"Wow. Can all of you teddies talk to humans?"

"Er, no, not really. No. Only some teddies, like me. I talk to Simon and Joanne and, well, I left dem now."

Teddy felt a pang in his tummy again, only made worse when Gruff interjected.

"You USED to have a master, and you LEFT him?"

There were definite traces of anger in Gruff's voice that even Teddy couldn't ignore.

"Yes. No. Yes ... oh!"

"What is it then? Did you leave your master?"

"He wasn't my master, really."

"But you LEFT him?"

"Um, yes."

"How could you *do* that? That's the very *worst* thing a dog can do!" snapped Gruff, and then realised his mistake. "Which, of course, you aren't. Hm."

They stared at each other. Gruff trying to control his outrage, and Teddy trying to understand why he suddenly felt like crying.

"Right. Well, maybe it's different for teddies, but don't you need to be part of something? How can you feel useful unless you're part of something? Unless you doing something useful *for* someone?"

"Don't know, I have dis ffingy that I've got to do. It's like a ffingy I'm following. It's the only ffingy I got to do in the whole world, and I keep thinking about it and it ... it ... makes me do it, I have to find her. I have no choice. I wanted ffings to stay the same at home, but day didn't!"

Gruff looked at him with a slightly softened expression, realising that Teddy was not master-less on a whim, and perhaps he didn't like it that way.

"Okay, calm down. Let's try to sort this out ... yes, listen: there might be someone else you can see, someone very old who knows this land, and the lands nearby, better than any human. He's also wise enough that he'll help you fix things, if you're making a big mistake."

Teddy nodded slowly, not entirely convinced that he wanted to meet someone who might try to talk him out of his plans, but he realised Gruff meant well. "Ffank you. Who is he?"

"He's a *very* old ram. Some say he's a story, a myth, but I've seen him: well, it was hazy, I was hurt. He helped me. I'm certain he would help you, and we're heading towards some sheep who can take you to meet him. The problem is, he's quite a long way away, and you'll have to convince the sheep that you can be trusted."

"Oh, dat's easy, because I *can* be trusted."

"Yes, but you'll have to *convince* them that you're not a threat and can be trusted."

"But dat's peesy eesy, I'll tell dem dat I'm Teddy so they know I can be trusted."

Gruff closed his eyes and sighed.

"You know, if anyone can make that work, it's you, Teddy."

"Ffank you!"

The conversation ebbed, and the companions gazed over the sides of the trailer at the passing countryside. They passed a house. Then another. Then a whole row of houses, opposite a caravan park, and they were driving into a small village square with a boarded-up public toilet block. Next, some shops, and the Landrover paused at a crossroads in the middle of the village. The village clock tower struck one o'clock as they turned left, then on through the shops, past an ironmonger's, a tiny police station, a garage, and some more houses, then some cottages, and they were out of the village and back into the countryside.

"Is it a long way to Ll-thhtht-clcllcclltht—"

"Llandegley?" offered Gruff, helpfully.

"Yes, dat."

"No, not really. Maybe fifteen or twenty minutes."

Soon they found themselves talking about Gruff and his job as a sheepdog, and how his entire family for generations had been sheepdogs, as far back as anyone could remember, and what being a sheepdog meant, and how he loved what he did and respected his master, backed up with several anecdotes demonstrating what an admirable, hardworking human his master was, and how he worked well with his master, and how they were both fair to the sheep, and then more anecdotes dealing with how silly and annoying sheep can be.

Then the conversation turned to Teddy, and Teddy found he didn't have much to say. He'd been made in a factory in Vietnam, he'd briefly woken up in a big basket full of other teddies in a shop, and he'd gone to live with Simon and Joanne. They'd had Bertie and suddenly Teddy wasn't wanted any more, so when he saw Lady Teddy, and found a purpose to his life, he'd left. That was his whole life. There was no history, no background, no rightful place in a family of other teddies, only that. And then Teddy stopped talking because he didn't feel like saying anything anymore, and he found himself looking at the matted, muddy fur on his leg paws, and wishing Gruff would say something.

Gruff nudged Teddy with his cold, wet, black nose. He understood Teddy a little better now.

"Hey! It'll be fine! You seem like a good teddy to me. Not that I've met many, I suppose. But you seem honest and genuine. I'm sure you'll find the old ram I mentioned, Ramgar. He'll tell you how to get to Clehonger, and you'll be with your Lady Teddy."

As he was saying the words, Gruff's tone of voice betrayed his real belief that Teddy was doomed to a very depressing, abject failure of a journey, but he was trying to be positive. His subsequent doggy smile was very forced.

"Oh ffank goodness!" said Teddy, relieved, and completely oblivious to any of this. "I was really starting to get a bit worried! Silly me!"

A minute later, in the small village of Llandegley, the

Landrover slowed and turned left onto a rocky track to the left of a farmhouse. The track snaked up the hill behind the farmhouse, ending halfway up the hill where three fields met.

"We're here," said Gruff. "That's the farmhouse and I've got to go to work in a minute. Here's what you need to do ..."

Gruff told Teddy how he would need to jump out of the trailer before they stopped at the top of the hill, so his master wouldn't find him. Gruff would help Teddy out of the moving trailer with his nose. After that, Teddy should run and hide under the nearest hedge and wait there until Gruff and his master had gone off with the sheep that they'd gather. Teddy should then find the other sheep and say, *"Gruff has told me to tell you to take me to Ramgar, because I am his friend."*

Teddy's eyes opened wide and he smiled. He had a friend! Then he realised that the only friend he had in the whole world was soon going to disappear down a muddy, stony lane, never to be seen again, with a trailer full of sheep, and he'd be left in a wet, Welsh field with a few sheep he didn't know at all. His smile disappeared.

"It's been nice talking to you Teddy," said Gruff, "I still think you're mad, but you're a good sort. Shame we couldn't have got to know each other better."

"Ffank you, Gruff! You too!"

They were at the jumping off point.

"Right, GO!" urged Gruff.

Teddy tried to scramble up the metal sides of the trailer with minimal success. He was slipping back down when he felt Gruff's nose push his bottom higher and higher. Teddy reached the tipping point and tumbled over the top, hit the ground and rolled and rolled on the hard stony track until he came to a stop. He glanced up and saw Gruff panting over the side of the trailer, with melancholy eyes, bouncing slightly as the trailer rolled into potholes and over cobbles. Gruff drove away and up the hill and Teddy successfully remembered that he had to hide under the hedge, so he did.

At the top, the trailer stopped next to a cattle box. Gruff's owner got out and opened up the trailer ready for Gruff to get out, and the two farmers greeted each other in Welsh and were soon chatting, laughing and joking. Teddy watched and waited. After a while, Gruff's master called him out of the trailer and unbolted the gate into the field, then he and Gruff began to herd the sheep. Between them they expertly drove the sheep down the field through the gate and into the waiting sheep trailer. The farmer unhooked the small metal trailer in which Teddy had travelled, and hooked up the sheep trailer in its place. Both farmers smiled and shook hands. It seemed a fair exchange had been made. They chatted some more, obviously not in any rush. Gruff's master opened the rear Landrover door and Gruff jumped up into the back. The farmers continued to laugh together and Teddy wished they'd just get this over with, which eventually they did. Gruff's master got in, the Landrover started up and they turned around in the space at the top of the track, then down, getting noisier and noisier as they came closer to Teddy. There was a splash of puddles and a crunching of stones as it drove by, and then the sounds began to subside. With a woof and a single howl, muffled by the window, Gruff said a sad goodbye to his friend. The Landrover reached the bottom of the hill by the farmhouse, and seconds later it turned right onto the main road and disappeared out of view.

Sometimes even a few minutes with someone is enough to make you miss them for the rest of your life; Teddy felt that truth at this moment.

- Chapter 4 -

Teddy And The Flock

"Be' wyt ti'n 'naed eh? Maaah!" said a voice from behind the hedge.

"Huh?" said Teddy.

"Beth. Rwyt. Ti'n. Gwnaed? Maaah!" It repeated, patronisingly slowly. It was a sheep.

"Um. I don't ffink I speak 'sheep'," said Teddy.

"Oh, you're English. Maaah. Most sheepdogs are first-language Welsh you know."

"Um. I'm not very Englishy, actchuley, I'm from Vietnam, and I'm a teddy!"

"A what?" queried the sheep, not even bleating.

"I'm a teddy!" said Teddy.

"Maaah. Come up to the gate where I can see you," grumped the sheep.

So Teddy did, and the sheep was clearly surprised at what she saw.

"Oh. You're ... a teddy, maaah. I've heard of teddies but ..." the sheep turned around, "MAAAAAAROOOOOOOON," she bleated out, loudly.

The flock peered over at Teddy and the sheep, forgetting their grass for a moment, but soon returned to their munching. However, one very solid looking sheep, presumably Maaroon, began to trot her way through the flock towards the odd pair at the gate. She didn't appear to be in any rush, but she was as surprised as her compatriot to see a teddy bear at their gate.

"Well, Maalaw, what do we have here then? Maaah" said

37

Maaroon, when she finally got to the gate.

"Maaah, he says he's a 'teddy'. I thought he was a dog, but actually he's—"

"Not, maaah," said Maaroon, cutting her off gently, with a smile. "Indeed."

She looked Teddy up and down. She trotted left and examined one side; trotted right, and examined the other, and then she looked at him again from the front.

"Maaah. You really *are* a teddy. I've only heard tales of 'teddies', and yet you seem to be one. Maaah. So what are we going to do with you?"

"Um, take me to ... Ramgar?" proffered Teddy, hopefully.

Both sheep gasped and their mouths dropped. Sheep nearby that had been eavesdropping, stopped eating, stared at him and their mouths fell open too. Within a couple of seconds, the whole flock was looking right at Teddy, either looking surprised at what he had said, or wondering what they'd missed.

"What?" asked Maaroon, looking both worried and a little annoyed.

Teddy was unnerved by their response. A few hours ago, he would have blustered on with a smile on his face, but after today's events Teddy's once happy-go-lucky attitude was not what it was. He was beginning to learn that sometimes it's better to think before you speak. He tried to remember what Gruff had said. He thought and thought. Nothing came. Then he realised. Gruff! That was it!

"Gruff said I should ask you."

Maaroon's look became marginally less stormy, but there was still deep concern in her voice when she spoke: "Did you know that no one outside The Flock should use the name of Ramgar? His name is special. Maaah. His name is special to us, here, in The Flock. Maaah. He is of Old Llandegley, and we, maaah, are some of the few that appreciate that. Maaah."

The mention of 'Llandegley' acted as a trigger to the other

sheep. Instead of standing and looking at Teddy, nearby sheep who had heard Maaroon speak quietly filed towards the gate; sheep from a distance followed too, without really understanding why, since that's what sheep do, and they all gathered behind Maaroon, and inspected Teddy.

"Um. What's dis Ll-thth-clclcclcc—"

"Llandegley," said Maalaw, the first sheep who'd seen Teddy, "is this place. It is very old. Maybe as old as the rocks and stones. We remember its traditions, maaah, while other sheep do not. You are not a sheep. You should not be talking of 'Ramgar' or 'Llandegley' or any other Flock matter that is not of your concern."

"Maaah. Thank you Maalaw," said Maaroon kindly, but firmly. But Maalaw was not finished. She closed her eyes and began:

"Llandegley is a Special Place."

"A Special Place," said Maaroon, automatically joining in and looking skywards.

"A Special Place," said Maalaw, nodding slowly and meaningfully.

A pause.

"Llandegley *is* a Special Place," she repeated, in a more hushed voice.

"And So Is My Whole Flock! MAAAH!" bleated the whole flock with all the air in their lungs, so amazingly loudly that Teddy nearly fell over.

Teddy got the feeling that this ritual wasn't quite right, somehow, and Maaroon seemed slightly embarrassed at her Lieutenant's initiative.

Teddy stared at the sheep. The sheep stared back at him.

"But Gruff said I could—"

"Gruff," said Maalaw, "should know better, maaah."

"Maaah. He should," agreed Maaroon. "Nevertheless, we all know Gruff has the respect of The Flock." Maaroon looked around;

the other sheep bleated quietly to each other in agreement. "So, we will listen, until you have spoken further."

"Then we may have to trample on you until your stuffing comes out," added Maalaw.

"Huh-wah?" spluttered Teddy, "KILL ME?"

"Well, yes, that's the law. Maaah. You can't just go about saying, 'Ramgar' and 'Llandegley', maaah!"

Maaroon tried to regain some balance.

"That is a very old law, Maalaw. We shall see what happens. Gruff has the respect of The Flock; he helped protect The Flock, at severe cost to himself; Gruff has been touched by Ramgar, and The Flock has sworn to respect him. Maaah. If Gruff truly has given you his name to use then we will at least listen. Now, please tell us your tale."

Teddy gulped. He didn't have a tail, only paws; maybe they'd understand if he told them what Gruff had said? Were they serious about trampling on him if he didn't convince them? After all, they were behind a gate and, although there were many of them, they were silly sheep, what could they do?

"Gruff is my ffrend, and he said dat you should take me to der Ramgar, because I need his help."

"Ah, so it's *help* you need? Maaah," said Maaroon, thoughtfully. "Hm. Of course, it's possible Ramgar *might* help you, but before any of that we need to make sure you're not dangerous, maaah, we need to know your motivations, maaah; although, obviously it's not like you're a wolf, or a bear, but—"

"I *am* a bear," said Teddy, unhelpfully.

"MAAAAAAAHH! MAAAAAAAAH! A BEAR! A BEAR!" panicked Maalaw.

There was chaos. The Flock ran in all directions, bumping into each other and falling over. Then scrambling up in a panic, only to bump into each other again.

"MAAAAH! PLACES!" shouted Maaroon.

It worked. Within moments, the flock had lined up into three neat rows of about ten sheep each. Maalaw, stood in front of them in a row of her own, facing Maaroon, and Maaroon took a breath and addressed them all.

"This creature is clearly not an ordinary bear. He is too small, too foolish, and he can talk. Also, he seems to be of limited intelligence. It doesn't seem likely he can harm us at all."

"I really am a bear," added Teddy, still not knowing when to be quiet.

Every muscle in every sheep in the flock twitched; they wanted nothing more than to run around bleating, but they managed to remain in formation.

"Maaah, well done. Despite the silliness of this creature, you have maintained the discipline I expect from The Flock. Very good. So, we'll now find out his true nature, and what he wants."

Maaroon turned to Teddy.

"So, explain yourself, teddy bear. Every detail. Every word you spoke with Gruff. Why are you here? How do you know him? What help do you want when you see Ramgar?"

Teddy was going to launch into a long set of answers when he felt something he'd never felt before. He was a little bit angry. Not very angry, just a little bit, but it was more angry than Teddy had ever been in his life, and he found himself becoming very unwilling to put up with the sheep in front of him. They were delaying him, and threatening him, and he was getting nowhere.

"No. I don't ffink I'm going to answer you. Everyone ffinks I'm der silly teddy, but I'm not! I am just trying to do my best, and my ffrend Gruff told me to TELL YOU to take me to Ramgar, and dat's what I ffink you is going to DO."

Teddy was more surprised than the sheep by what he'd said, but only just. Maaroon, studied him like a poker player trying to assess whether his opponent was bluffing, and finally she decided that this teddy was as serious as he could be.

"Maaah. Okay," she said.

"What?" said Teddy.

"MAAAH! WHAT?" said Maalaw.

Maaroon smiled, enjoying the obvious shock of what she'd said. "Seriously. It's fine. Maaah. I think this Teddy is harmless. Does it look like he could eat us? Or even attack us? Maaah. Where are his teeth? Could he hurt us with his padded arms?"

Maalaw was clearly not happy. If Maaroon noticed, she didn't let it show. She continued.

"In any case, we have good reason to trust Gruff, and the teddy has used Gruff's name. Maaah. We have not been to see Ramgar for a while, so we'll take Teddy with us and use it as an excuse to go now. It will be good for The Flock if you and I speak with Ramgar again. Maaah. It always changes us, and reminds us of what it means to be a part of The Flock."

"But our traditions clearly state that we should not take an Unflock anywhere *near* Ramgar!" insisted Maalaw.

"Gruff is an Unflock and he saved our lives, and went to Ramgar. I sometimes think we fear too much, and cling to tradition too easily, maaah, and trust too little. I am becoming more and more convinced that if our Way means anything then we should know when to trust those in need, rather than relying on protocol and threat. Maaah. If this teddy is harmful, Ramgar will see it and stop him; if he is honourable, then who are we to stand in his way?"

"Maaah," said Maalaw grumpily, not at all persuaded, but unable to do anything about it.

"So," said Maaroon. "We will take this wandering teddy to Ramgar, maaah. We will begin tomorrow at dawn, if ..." she smiled at Teddy, not entirely kindly, " ... you can get over this gate. Maaah."

Maalaw's eyes sparkled at this small concession to her.

The gate was twice Teddy's height. It was not going to be easy, but he didn't want to stay stuck in this lane, divided from these sheep who might help him. He tried to plan his ascent, then realised that he wasn't very good at planning. So he looked at his paws, to see which ones would start the climb. He chose his left leg paw and right arm paw.

To his surprise, he found his foot didn't slip on the metal of the gate. It was so matted with grit and grime that it gripped much better than he had expected. He stepped up and could now reach up with his left arm paw more than half way up the gate! Unfortunately, his arm paws were far less dirty, and he had trouble gripping the gate to pull himself up higher. There was a murmur of mocking 'maaah's from The Flock. Teddy found that he could wrap his left arm paw over the gate's bars and pull himself up one rung. His right paw similarly pushed down on its rung and his other arm paw was now nearly at the top rung of the gate. He tried to wrap his left arm paw over in the way he had done before, but it slipped and Teddy was immediately and unceremoniously dumped, bottom-first, onto the stones and mud of the lane. A roar of bleating met this failure as The Flock mocked his misfortune.

Teddy was not going to give up, however. He repeated his climb, and this time was very careful to get a firm hold with his left arm paw before putting all his weight on it. It was enough to pull him up to the top of the gate. He managed to wrap his head and snout over the top of the gate, and found himself looking straight at Maalaw, who did not look the least bit happy. Teddy windmilled his right paw over the top of the gate, then his left paw, and lost his grip again. His two leg paws paddled madly in mid-air, but this time he didn't fall because his right arm paw regained a firm enough hold, and eventually he found a foothold, and pushed his bottom sideways until it was the same height as his head on the top rung.

Now he had his arm paws and head on one side of the top of the gate, and his leg paws and bottom on the other side, and he was stuck. If he tried to move his legs he was in real danger of falling back again, because his legs were fully extended. Teddy realised that the only way down from the gate was to pull himself over with his arm paws and to simply fall off the gate onto the other side. So he did. He pulled on one arm paw until his head was lower than his bottom; then he pulled on the other arm paw, and he pulled some more, and began to fall over the gate, faster until he flipped over the top of gate and landed in a heap on the ground at Maaroon's feet.

"Maaah. You really want to see Ramgar don't you?"

"Yes, please!" said Teddy with some of his old bounciness, rubbing his shoulder.

Maalaw scowled and looked away.

"Come with me," said Maaroon, showing her teeth in a sheep smile before she began to walk away.

Teddy picked himself up and followed her; Maalaw fell in behind Teddy, grumbling and bleating under her breath.

Maaroon explained that they would be travelling all day tomorrow and probably part of the next day too. First, however, she would need to make sure The Flock would be well cared for while she was away.

It didn't take long to tell Teddy all this, perhaps five minutes, and it would have taken considerably less time if Teddy had not had difficulty understanding some of the things she was saying, then she left Teddy to himself while made the Flock ready for her absence.

Teddy spent the rest of that day wandering around the field, trying to talk to sheep (who just looked nervous and ran away) and taking other measures to stave off boredom. It turns out that teddies can't eat grass, walk properly on all four paws or jump very high. However, he got a bit better at climbing the gate after practicing several times. It seemed like the longest day of Teddy's life, and all the while he was desperate to get going to find Lady Teddy. It was very frustrating. There was nothing to do, nothing useful with which to occupy his time, and Teddy was lonely and missed Simon and Joanne, and even baby Bertie. He was beginning to wonder what he was doing here, in the middle of a field, miles from home.

Eventually, it began to get dark.

"Maaaaah!" bleated Maalaw to Maaroon, "It is the time to sleep now."

"Maaah. You are right Maaroon. Thank you," and she bleated particularly loudly, in a slightly unusual way, and The Flock began to settle down for the night.

"Um. We going to sleepy *here*? In der field?"

"Yes, of course. Maaah," smiled Maalaw, unkindly, beginning her bedtime snack. "Iffff dare a broblem?" she munched.

"I never slept in a field before. Actchuley, I never slepts out of a *house* before!"

"Maaah. Oh beer," crunched Maalaw, deliberately unconvincing in her sympathy, eating her pre-sleep supper hungrily.

Teddy searched for shelter. It was twilight and he couldn't see very far, and the trees and bushes were looking increasingly black and scary.

The best 'bed' he could find was find a reasonably dry patch of hard earth underneath part of the field's hedge. He wiggled and wiggled to get in place, but his head still stuck out. He decided it was better than nothing, so he lay there in his bed made of hedge. At least it was a pleasantly warm summer evening.

Teddy closed his eyes and imagined he was far away from these sheep. He thought about Lady Teddy and smiled, but soon found his thoughts drifting away to his old home and his old family, and he felt a chill in the depths of his stuffing. Teddy's thoughts rambled on for an hour or so, but eventually he fell asleep.

::

The next morning, Teddy woke up looking straight up at the sky. It was confusing. Why was he outside? Where was his sleeping-chair? Then he remembered it all.

Maalaw loomed into view above him, slightly to his right.

"Maaah. Can you roll?" she asked?

"Huh?" said Teddy, sleepily.

"Can you *roll*, maaah," repeated Maalaw, "yes, or no?"

"Um, yes. I ffink."

"We'll soon see. You'll need to, if we are to meet Ramgar."

As Teddy wiggled out of the bush and sat up, Maaroon joined them, asked how Teddy had slept and explained that their journey would be in three stages: (i) along the road for a few miles; (ii) a trek up into the hills, and then (iii) the descent down into England.

First, however, there was to be the 'Handing Over'. Teddy had no idea was this was, but it soon became clear it was a highly formal ceremony in which Maaroon and Maalaw, and their temporary replacements, trotted up and down the field to various places, where they ritualistically ate patches of grass, and spoke about how The Flock is important, and how it needs good leaders, and how they were willing to hand over authority for a while. It seemed to Teddy to take forever.

There was much bowing of heads and murmured bleating, but at last Maaroon and Maalaw completed the ceremony with the 'touching of noses', at which point the temporary transfer of leadership was complete. The ritual was over and the sheep slowly went back to milling around the field, eating.

Maaroon trotted over to Teddy.

"It's time to go, teddy bear."

There was an odd look in her eye that Teddy didn't quite understand: it was as if she was trying to remember something. It only lasted a moment, then she turned to go, indicating with a move of her head that Teddy should follow.

Even their leaving was formal. Apparently, it was Maalaw's job to open a gap in the hedge, and the other sheep watched as she expertly performed her task. Maaroon and Maalaw bowed to their replacements, and to the rest of the flock, and then they wiggled through the hedge, followed by Teddy.

::

The journey 'along the road' wasn't very close to the road at all.
Sometimes they could hardly see it, or hear the cars. However, the
road was their guide for this part of the journey, so when the road
bore left, so did they, and when the road swept right, they went that
way too.

The sheep didn't particularly make an effort to talk to Teddy,
they strode ahead and he had to do his best to keep up with them,
half-walking, half-running, so he had little choice but to watch them
from behind. After an hour, Teddy noticed that Maaroon and
Maalaw were very different. Maaroon seemed calm, relatively
approachable and thoughtful; she was busy making sure they went
the right way, but occasionally stopped to smell the warm summer
air and look at the view. She glanced back at Teddy every few
minutes but said nothing.

Maalaw, however, was more concerned that they should do
everything 'right', and made it her job to tell Maaroon whenever
there was a point of order that needed addressing. She would say
when it was time for a formal meal; she would point out that they
were walking 'the wrong way' round a field; she would note when
they had taken too many steps without pausing to bleat (apparently
it's not 'Flock-like' to walk continuously). She almost never made
eye contact with Teddy.

Teddy was intrigued and tried to work out why she was so
concerned with these things. After thinking about it for a mile or so,
he jogged up to her and asked.

"Why do you like all der 'have to's?"

"Shh, maaah, I'm counting."

"Huh?"

"I'm countin— MAAAH! Now I've lost count."

Both Maaroon and Maalaw stopped, almost as one. Maaroon
turned to face Maalaw and looked kindly at her, but said nothing.

Maalaw gave a sharp, annoyed sigh.

"I was counting our footsteps. It's not acceptable to walk too far in one go. Since we are of The Flock, we have to be examples to other sheep."

Maaroon dropped her gaze and smiled before looking up and interjecting to smooth things over.

"Maalaw is the guardian of the ways of our Flock, and she is very good at it. She takes it very seriously."

"Of course I do! Maaah!" snapped Maalaw, apparently annoyed that she should be considered 'serious'. "The Flock is the only thing between us and death. Maaah. These rules protect us and keep us safe; we must *never* forget that. Maaah."

"There is a lot of truth in that," agreed Maaroon, diplomatically, "Yet, I'm sure you'll agree there is more to The Flock than rules?"

"Well, yes, of course. I suppose," stumbled Maalaw. "However, obedience to The Way must always come first."

Maaroon smiled, "And with you to care for us, it always will. Maaah. Thank you for keeping us on the safe path."

"Should *I* count my feet too?" asked Teddy, not quite understanding.

"Not your feet, maah; the number of steps your feet take on the ground," grumped Maalaw. "And no, you shouldn't, because you are not of The Flock."

"Oh dear! Can I be in der flock? I want to be safe too!"

"No, you cannot. You are a teddy. We are sheep. Even most other sheep reject our Way, maaah. How could *you* possibly follow The Way then? Maaaah."

Maalaw stomped off.

"Don't worry Teddy," added Maaroon. "You'll be safe travelling with us, maaah."

"Oh, dat's good, cos actchully I don't ffink I'm very good at counting."

"Just think peaceful thoughts, and let Maalaw look after us. I will take us where we need to go. You will need to calm your mind if you want to be allowed to see Ramgar."

Although Teddy was sure Maaroon was trying to be helpful, he was now more worried than ever. As they trudged along, tracking the road Teddy tried to imagine what Ramgar might be like. Would he be *really* big, with huge horns? Would he be angry and loud? What would he do to Teddy? How could Teddy calm his mind with thoughts like these?

Teddy gave up. Since Maalaw was not able to talk to him, because she was counting, Teddy ran ahead to talk to Maaroon.

"Don't you count your feet?" asked Teddy.

Maaroon smiled, "No I don't. I suppose I stop when it feels sheep-like to do so, maaah. Or when Maalaw tells me to." Her eyes twinkled, naughtily. "Although Maalaw is right that we need The Way to keep us safe, maaah, there is more to life than rules. The Way keeps us safe so that we can discover life, maaah; it helps us make others happy; it's helps us find peace, maaah." She quickly trotted nearer to Teddy and spoke into his ear, "I don't want my Flock to lose these things."

Teddy was surprised. She had trusted him with her concern. Behind, Maalaw was counting under her breath, looking grimly at the ground.

They walked for hours, stopping and starting according to The Way. Teddy might have minded the continual delays if it were not for the fact that he could hardly keep up with the sheep when they were moving, and he needed the rest.

"Did you know, Teddy, there are more sheep in Wales than people? Maaah," asked Maaroon, while they were stopped again.

"Really?"

"Really. A lot more. Maaah. Yet humans have taken over the land, and built houses and farms, maaah, and their roads and hedges and tracks are everywhere."

Teddy looked around. It was true. He'd never seen it like that before. He imagined what the land would look like without the things that people had made. It seemed quite pleasant, although he did rather like people, and didn't want them to disappear. His lonely ache returned again.

"We will reclaim our land! Maaah!" asserted Maalaw, forcefully.

"Maybe we will, maaah" mused Maaroon slowly, "But that was not my point."

"What was your point then? Maaah!" asked Maalaw, grumpily, eating grass as they paused one more.

"Only that Teddy should see things differently. Maaah. Sometimes, when you change how you see *one* thing, maaah, *other* thoughts can change and move too, maaah, like the wind can bend a field of grass blades.

Maalaw didn't know what to make of this kind of talk.

They continued walking, but this time they headed straight for the road. Maalaw performed her duty and cleared a new hole for them in the field's hedge, and they were through to the other side, standing on the verge by the side of the road.

"Maaah. Now we will see if you can roll," said Maaroon, with a genuine smile, and she directed Teddy's gaze a few metres up the road to a cattle grid.

"So far, we have avoided people completely, and we have avoided the road as much as possible, maaah, but we now need to get over there." She pointed with a hoof to the other side of the cattle grid. "Maaah, and this is how we do it."

Maaroon, waked up to the cattle grid, lay down, stuck all four legs out to one side, and rolled to the other side of the gridded bars. It seemed to hurt her because it took her a while to get back up onto her hooves when she reached the other side, and she was stiff and awkward. Once she was standing again, her gentle pride returned to her face and she indicated to Maalaw to follow her. She did, and also winced.

Once both sheep were on the other side it was Teddy's turn. Both sheep watched with interest.

Teddy sat down on his bottom by the edge of the cattle grid, lay down and rolled. Bump, one, bump, two, bump, three, bump, four, bump, five, bump, six; six bars of the cattle grid. He stood up and smiled.

"Did it!" he smiled. The sheep were amazed.

"Maaah. It takes months of practice for a sheep to do that! No sheep has ever managed to roll first time, and yet you smile." Maalaw, was in danger of showing respect, and she knew it.

"Ffank you! But I don't ffink teddies find rolling very hard, actchully cos we're squashy."

"You really are a wonderfully strange, surprising creature, Teddy," said Maaroon.

They left the road at the moment a stream of traffic came into view: a slow car pulling a caravan, with ten or twelve cars behind it. The drivers were too annoyed with their lack of speed to see a teddy bear pressing himself through a gap in the hedge to catch up with two sheep.

The climb into the hills was uneventful, but Teddy noticed the fields gradually became more rocky, and the grass became patchier. Maalaw complained that this really wasn't "Flock land," but little else was said. They just walked for miles in silence, and almost all the time it was uphill and slow. Teddy's short legs ached more than they had done in his entire life, and the sheep became frustrated by how slowly Teddy walked. It annoyed Maalaw particularly intensely. Even Teddy was frustrated with himself that it was taking so long to get to Ramgar.

Whenever they reached a hedge, Teddy would look from left to right trying to see a gap. Then Maalaw would push in just the right place to make a hole for them. He asked how she kept managing to find weak spots in hedges and Maalaw told him (with great pride) that it was a gift of The Flock. It allowed them to roam where they wanted, and to escape being taken to market, and she went on to say that the thing that made her most proud was that none of The Flock had human markings on their backs.

Finally, they reached the highest point on their journey, a pass between two hills. It was made spectacular by the sun setting behind them, and Teddy kept glancing over his shoulder to look at the gorgeous red and purple colours of the darkening sunset.

"It is time to stop for the night," said Maalaw formally. Maaroon nodded and both she and Maalaw began their bedtime meal, ready to settle down.

This time, Teddy found an excellent place to sleep: a hut, down in a dip by the field's hedge. He scurried over to it, now oblivious to the mud and warm puddles through which he was splashing, because his leg paws simply couldn't get any more dirty or wet than they already were. He was getting used to feeling a continual, deep dampness in his leg stuffing.

The hut was a store for animal feed. There were three or four bales of hay, some buckets, a split water-butt and a rusty fork with a spike missing. It was a mess, but it looked wonderful to Teddy.

After thinking for a while, he managed to jam the door shut with the fork and climbed onto the highest bale and lay down. He was exhausted from the climb, and within three minutes he was fast asleep and snoring.

- Chapter 5 -

Teddy And The Circle

He awoke the next morning to hear Maalaw kicking the hut door alternately with each of her front legs.

"MAAAAH! WAKE UP!"

"Ughhgh," groaned Teddy, still not fully awake, and wondering what was happening. However, today, it took less time for him to remember where he was and what was going on.

"WAKE UP! Maaah, I've been kicking this door quite long enough. It's time to GO! MAAAAH!"

"Uh-oh. Oh dear! I was tired! Awake now, though!" said Teddy, surprisingly jolly about the whole thing.

It took him a while to remove the fork from the door because Maalaw's kicking had dug it into the ground and it had become jammed under one of the door's cross pieces, but once that was done soon he was out of the hut.

It was much cooler today and, more importantly, it was raining. Maaroon was eating, but she lifted her head and nodded a greeting at Teddy while she chewed.

"It's raining," Teddy mused, to no one in particular.

"Is that a problem?" said Maalaw.

"Um, I don't ffink Teddies can get wet."

"Then teddies can't go to see Ramgar!" she gloated.

Teddy was in a difficult position; here he was, in the rain, on top of some hills in the middle of nowhere, with no way back. Moreover, he could only go forward if he went with these sheep.

"Have to try den," he said, stoically.

"Maaah. Come on Teddy," encouraged Maaroon, after

finishing her meal. "We're moving on," and she began to walk toward an apparently impenetrable stretch of hedge with Maalaw behind her.

The rain was falling fast and hard. Within ten minutes, Teddy was soaking wet to the middle of his stuffing, and something rather odd began to happen. He felt Sleepy. Not a tired kind of sleepy, but the kind of Sleepy-with-a-capital-S you feel when no one loves you and you're a teddy. The kind of Sleepy that leads to a teddy falling Asleep. Teddy fought it hard, but there was no denying he needed to find someone to love him fairly quickly or he would be Asleep, perhaps in the middle of a field. Soon he would look like a bloated wet, muddy rat, with stuffing that would become the perfect home for mice. Then he would be ripped open by inquisitive birds looking for nesting material, and eventually, he would be in pieces all over the country, dead.

Obviously, such thoughts did not exactly encourage Teddy, but luckily it took him over two miles of walking to finally reach these conclusions, and by that time the rain had stopped and the sun was trying to come out. It didn't succeed, but at least the rain didn't return, so Teddy slowly began to dry out. As he dried, the Sleepiness receded slightly.

By now, the track had dropped down a long way from the ridge where they had slept, and they were getting close to roads and houses and farms again. Of concern to both sheep was that they would have to walk near fields of other sheep.

"Why does dat matter?" asked Teddy.

"Because these sheep are not Flock sheep. Not even slightly. They are stupid, vacuous sheep that live to eat, maaah. And then are taken away by farmers and—"

"Thank you Maalaw, that's quite graphic enough," interjected Maaroon. "She's right, though, Teddy. These are not our friends, maaah. We must be careful."

So they took their time, looking for fields that were empty.

Teddy helped by climbing onto Maaroon's back to look over the top of some of the shorter hedges. He also used his new gate-climbing skills to look further than they could see from the ground, although he still tumbled off a couple of times.

They crossed empty fields and roads, and even walked along quiet lanes to avoid fields of non-Flock sheep. Eventually, however, they they were challenged at a gate by a tough-looking sheep.

"Who the 'ell are you? Baaa. You're not from these parrrts, whatcha dooin'?"

Then it saw they had no markings and realised.

"FLOCK SHEEP! FLOCK SHEEP 'ERE! BAAA!"

Teddy, Maaroon and Maalaw turned and bolted along the road until they were well clear of the field.

"Why did day sound diffrent?" asked Teddy, panting.

"We're almost in England now," said Maalaw, actually being helpful. "They say, 'Baaa' here, which is not right at all. Maaah. The Way has passed down to us that we should make a soft, natural 'maaah' sound, not their hard 'baaa' sound. Maaah."

"I'm not a sheep, but I'm glad I'm with your flock, not theirs."

"Oh. Thank you Teddy," said Maalaw. She may have wanted to find a point of order, but if she managed to think of one, she didn't mention it. Her expression was almost kind.

"So deez sheep don't like Ramgar den?" checked Teddy.

"Not really, no, maaah," said Maaroon. "The few that do accept he exists mostly think he's got nothing useful to say. Maaah. They merely want to eat as much grass as they can before they die."

"Oh dear," said Teddy. Then he thought, "So why does Ramgar live *here* den? If you is all in Cll-ccc-thlllan—"

"Llandegley," said Maalaw, almost patiently.

"Yes, dare. If you is dare den why is Ramgar here?"

"Because he wants to spread The Way here. Maaah. These sheep, or their lambs, or their lambs' lambs must learn to live according to The Way, maaah."

"What if day don't want to?" asked Teddy.

"Well, they must. Maaah," snapped Maalaw, returning to her less helpful demeanour, and she walked off.

"You know, Teddy, you answered that question yourself, maaah," added Maaroon, coming alongside Teddy and walking with him. "You said you were glad to be with us, not them. Maaah. That's why they need The Way too."

Teddy thought he understood, a little bit. Nevertheless, living in the outside world was a *lot* more complicated than he had realised.

::

Their journey took them nearer to human settlements, but they were not seen, or at least no one bothered them.

Eventually, they entered a wood near Whitney Court, and both Maaroon and Maalaw became noticeably more tense.

"Soon, we will try to meet Ramgar, at The Circle, maaah," said Maaroon, nervously. "If he agrees to see us, maaah, then we'll speak with him first, and we'll ask him if he'll see you. If we are successful, he will invite you in. Speak only when he speaks to you, maaah. And kneel, too."

Both sheep were extremely nervous now, and a few minutes later they reached a mass of tall, thick fir trees, with branches to the ground. They had grown together into a circle, or perhaps they had been planted there by humans, or perhaps there was some other explanation, but there they were. A circle of trees, deep in a wood, with no apparent way in.

"MAAAAAAAH!" called Maaroon.

"MAAAAAAAAAAAAAH!" called Maalaw, even louder.

"MAAAAAAAAAAAAAAAAAAH!" they bleated together.

They listened. A bird flapped out of a tree. A small animal rustled and escaped through the undergrowth, completely terrified by the noise.

There was a faint sound of cars on a distant road.

Then a voice boomed from inside The Circle, "COME! MAAAAAAH!" It was deep, dark, and yet there was a warmth about it. Maaroon and Maalaw quickly trotted up to the circle and found a way through. They glanced at each other for support, and they disappeared through the opening into the trees, leaving Teddy alone in the wood.

There were murmurs, noises, talking. At first it was calm, then he heard Maalaw saying something more forcefully, but she was cut-off halfway through by the deep, dark, calm voice. Maaroon then spoke at length, but she was too muffled for Teddy to make out the words. The voices returned to murmurs for a while, then Maalaw squeezed outside of the circle again. She looked sheepishly at the ground when she spoke.

"Ramgar would like you to enter The Circle to talk to him. You can come this way." Her tone was gentle, helpful, almost kind again. It made Teddy smile at her. A genuine, happy smile because she was being nice to him. He pushed his way through the tree at the place Maalaw showed him, and entered The Circle. Maalaw followed.

It was not as dark in The Circle as Teddy had expected. The tops of the trees did not join, and it allowed light to flood down to the forest floor. In the middle was a ram. A very old ram. He appeared brown and shrivelled, like a very large woolly raisin with horns: he was surely the oldest ram that there has ever been. Despite his elderly appearance, even a human would not have dared challenge him.

On his left and right were groups of three Blacksheep, standing in a line; they appeared to be his attendants or guards. Teddy wondered if Ramgar actually lived here. It was an odd place, with no comforts, and no edible grass, just an earthy, mossy floor and a single brown, circular stone in the centre, on which Ramgar stood.

"Maaah. You are a teddy?" said Ramgar, his smooth, slightly

surprised voice not at all suiting his aged body.

"Dat's me!" said Teddy, trying to get onto one knee, but failing because he didn't really have any knees. So he sat on his bottom instead.

"A real teddy! Well, this is a surprise. I think it's a good one; at least, I hope it is. Maaroon has told me about you. It's so interesting to meet someone ... diff-er-ent." Ramgar pronounced every syllable carefully and with great warmth. "Especially since I hear you want to see me! Maaah!"

"Yes, please!" said Teddy, "I mean, ffank you. A lot."

Teddy paused. Ramgar said nothing.

Teddy wiggled on his bottom to get comfortable on the hard ground. Ramgar still said nothing. Teddy glanced at Maaroon, who looked confused, and then at Maalaw, who was still shell-shocked from whatever had happened during her talk with Ramgar.

Ramgar simply stood in the middle of The Circle staring kindly at Teddy, without a word.

Teddy spoke. "So, do you know where der Clehonger is den? Um, please?"

"I do," said Ramgar.

Teddy waited for the information, but it didn't come.

"Errr. Can you tell me how to get dare den, please?"

"Yes, I can," said Ramgar.

Another pause. Teddy couldn't work out what Ramgar wanted. He glanced around him to see if anyone could tell him that he was missing something, but by now everyone, even the Blacksheep, were looking confused.

"Do I need to *do* sumffing? You know, for you to tell me how to get to der Clehonger? Please, sir, ffank you?"

"Not really. I'm waiting."

"What for?"

"To see how you act under pressure, and for you to tell me *why* you need this information. You see, you have engaged a Flock. You have travelled for many hours with the leaders of that Flock, and you have found me and come to talk to me, here, in The Circle. These are not normal things. Some would say they are bad things. Some would say they are good. I am simply confused that a real teddy has come to see me. Maaah."

Several of the attending Blacksheep openly showed surprise at this admission from Ramgar. Surely he was not really confused? Ramgar continued.

"I am certain that many in The Flock would have been terrified of you, because many in The Flock are terrified of almost everything. Maaah! That is why we *need* The Flock. It brings security, and peace, and being *together*, so we can share who we are and feel the strength of The Flock. However, over time, it also brings small-mindedness and a love for ritual, plus the over-simplification of who is a friend and who is an enemy. Finally bigotry and violence permeate and take over. Maaah. I fear we will see more of these things as time passes. Maaah."

At this, Maalaw shifted awkwardly on her four feet.

"Yet, you managed to cut through it all! You met a Flock and within a few minutes you had persuaded their leaders to travel to see me! Maaah. So, I want to learn about you. I want to find out why you are here. I want to find out the *real* reasons for the things that have happened, because I want to learn. If I stop learning, then I become no more than a purveyor of rules and tradition myself, and that is *not* why I am here. I am here to help us stay strong and safe, and I want to know to whom I am talking, so I can decide whether I should help him. That is my price for giving you directions to where you wish to go, you must first direct *me*, to an understanding of who you are. Maaah. It's a fair transaction."

Teddy was not sure Ramgar was talking to the right person. He was Teddy, that's all; what else was there to say? Worse, he didn't understand much of what Ramgar had said, or how to answer him. Yet it seemed that he would have to try if he was going to get the information he needed. The only words that Teddy understood were when Ramgar asked, "*I want to learn about you. I want to find out why you are here.*" So, that's where Teddy began.

"So, er, I am a teddy. Dat's important to me. I'm not sure why, but I likes everyone to know dat! Um. I am trying to find der lovely Lady Teddy. She stopped outside my house, and no one seems to love me in my house any more. Actchully, I don't think it *is* my house now. But, when I saw der Lady Teddy, and saw 'Clehonger' on her car, I ffort I would try to finds her, and den I could be wiv her family, and I could belong again and have a friend who's a teddy who I could love, and who would love me too. So I left my house, and have been travelling ever since. Deez sheeps have been nice to me, and day have shown me how to get to you, and you're bein' quite nice to me, actchually, and I ffink you're going to tell me how to get to Clehonger?"

Ramgar's appearance changed slightly. His demeanour became a little older and sadder; like he had felt a pain and it was heavy on him, and he had to carry it while trying to remain in charge and strong.

"You have come all this way ... for love?"

"Um, I ffink so?"

"Hm. Not just a love that you hope to find, but also a love that you have lost. Maaah." He thought to himself for a moment. "Let me ask you another question."

"Yeah, okay."

"Let me ask you this — a test, if you will: if you were in a field of sheep, and a dog got into the field, and started to attack the sheep, what would you do?"

"I'd shout, "NO!" at der doggy, because dat's *not* nice, and der doggy should stops."

"And what if the dog did not stop?"

"I would run over to him and try to stop him! He would be a naughty doggy and he should stops!"

"And how would you stop him?"

"I'd ... I'd ... "

"Yes, go on. Remember, this dog is biting sheep; making them bleed, and hurting them."

"I'D GET HIM TO BITE ME INSTEAD! I'm only made of fluff and fur, but maybe he would leave dem alone. I don't know what else could I do? I'm a teddy, and teddies can't ... can't ... can't do very much!" Teddy's frustration and tiredness and confusion overflowed and he burst into tears. "I'm just a teddy, I can't do anything! I can't help anyone. I'm useless! I want to be loved by someone, and Lady Teddy is my only hope and I REALLY WANT TO FIND HER."

Teddy said no more. All he could do was sob, with his paw to his head, looking at the ground.

Ramgar blinked. Then slowly and calmly breathed in and out before he spoke.

"Listen to me, my friend. I think you're showing me who you are, with honesty, and I thank you. You've come a long way already, and it's clearly taking its toll on you, but you still have a fair way to go. Maaah. Let me tell you what you want to know. Are you ready? Maaah."

Teddy nodded between sobs.

"You start by walking to the river, just down from here, and you follow the flow of the river until you reach the Bredwardine Bridge. Then you need to cross the Bredwardine Bridge, which you must *only* do during the day. Follow the road left for a few miles and you will be in Moccasin territory. Be very careful, we hear odd things are happening in Moccas these days. From there, continue to follow the road, trying to avoid humans when you pass through their villages lest they try to enforce their will upon you. Then on and on along the road, until you reach Clehonger. If at any time you can walk near the road, rather than on the road, then do it. Human cars are vicious things that stop for no animal.

"Hm. I believe you will reach your destination; I am not sure, however, that it will reach you."

Teddy was confused by the last statement, but it was soon forgotten when he realised he had just been given all the information he needed to reach Lady Teddy's village.

"Remember, if things grow dark for you, your love and gentleness are your strengths, and there is not enough of either in this world. Maaah. I do not think it an exaggeration to say that we will not meet anyone like you again. You matter, Teddy. Your goodness affects those around you. I believe you are more important to us, than we yet realise."

Teddy wasn't sure that Ramgar was right, and it showed.

"I mean it! Let me put it another way. Some here believe The Way is love, and *enriching* those around them is the most important thing. Others believe The Way is a law that keeps loved ones safe; to them the *safety* of their Flock is the vital thing. Still others want no formal Way at all; they simply want freedom and sensation for their few years on this land.

"Perhaps in a way they are all correct, but you have passed among all three, you have stirred them all up like a stick through the bottom of a pond. Maaah. It is not your fault, but things are moving now. We will see what happens, both to you, and to them, but I think I know more about The Bear in front of me than even he does. Exceptional things will happen, Teddy."

Teddy thought it odd to hear someone call him a 'The Bear', not to mention the other things that Ramgar had said, but it didn't really register because he was distracted. All he could think about was how he was going to run down the river, and race along the road, and rush to Lady Teddy, and love her.

- Chaper 6 -

Teddy And The River

It was with great excitement that Teddy squeezed himself between prickled branches and out of The Circle, Maaroon and Maalaw following closely behind. Outside, they stood together awkwardly for a few seconds without a word. Neither sheep could look Teddy properly in the eye: Ramgar's words had changed how they saw him. Maaroon opened her mouth, as if to say something, but closed it again after a pause. In the end she just bleated a heartfelt farewell, nodded at Teddy, and turned to begin the long walk back to her Flock. Maalaw followed her leader's example, nodding a farewell, and she too was on her way.

Teddy hadn't expected this. He was still the same Teddy, why should they find it hard to talk to him? As he watched them leave, two of Ramgar's Blacksheep approached. The leader indicated with a slow motion of his head, in something like the manner of a butler, to turn and walk in the opposite direction.

Ramgar was right, it only took a couple of minutes to reach the river. The lead Blacksheep silently nodded him in the right direction, then they too turned around, disappeared into Whitney wood, and left him alone.

Standing there on the river bank, with the erratic, winding path in front of him, he realised that this was the first time in his life that he had been alone like this. Here he was, in the middle of a field in England, and there was no one else. Moreover, if he didn't find Lady Teddy, there might never be anyone else again. It was a bit unnerving, but he took comfort in Ramgar's words that he would be fine, or at least he thought that was what Ramgar had said. In any case, he was determined he was going to walk this path to find his Lady Teddy.

Teddy realised that he didn't know how long the journey would take, but Ramgar had said there was still quite a long way to go, so it sounded like he would need to find somewhere to sleep tonight. Would there be other nights? He had no idea. He was not only alone; he was homeless, for the moment at least. He remembered seeing a man beside Barclay's bank in town, back in Aberystwyth, begging for money. Simon had told him that he was homeless, and now Teddy was standing here just like that man. This was turning out to be quite a stuffing-churning day.

To make matters worse, Teddy was feeling Tired again. Tired with a capital-T because no one loved him, like he'd felt in the field with Maaroon and Maalaw. While he'd been with Ramgar, and to a lesser extent Maaroon, he had felt he could cope with it, but now he really needed to find Lady Teddy quickly, before he fell Asleep.

He drew comfort from the fact that the summertime sun wouldn't go down for a few hours yet. Teddy guessed he would cover quite a lot of ground before bedtime. He didn't like lying down on the ground and going to sleep, so he'd walk while he could.

He trudged on for an hour or so, following the curves of the river. To begin with, he thought Ramgar was silly for telling him to follow such a winding route, but began to realise that there were no humans on this side of the river, no houses, and no roads, so if he walked away from the river he might lose his way. The grass alone was almost as high as Teddy. Ramgar was wise.

A few minutes later he came to a small stream. To the left, water flowed in from the long, grassy fens; to the right, it widened slightly and joined the river. There was no choice, he had to wade into the stream. With each step, the water rose higher and higher until it was up to the bottom of his tummy. It was cold, and in his Tired state drenching the bottom half of his body only made things worse, but the stream bed began to rise and soon he was up and standing on the other side of the water.

He walked on. At first his wet legs bothered him, cold in the cooling evening, but after an hour they were almost dry. Unfortunately, he soon had to cross another stream, and then he found he was travelling back towards Ramgar because the river had curved around completely at this point. For a further half an hour he had to walk *away* from Lady Teddy, getting grumpier all the time. Moreover, the light was dulling and dusk approached.

At last, the river curved around again, and he walked half an hour the other way, until he was almost back where he started. It was beginning to get quite dark now; Teddy was very frustrated and increasingly Tired, which slowed his pace.

"I better find a place to sleepy," he thought.

On the other side of the river was a cottage, set back from the riverbank. The lights were on and the windows open in an attempt to let the freshening air blow the heat of the day from its rooms. People were laughing inside, and Teddy thought it sounded like the plinks and clanks of someone making supper. He thought about Simon and Joanne at home with baby Bertie, eating and laughing and hugging and going to sleep, and his stuffing ached. Did they miss him even a little bit? But they were gone, miles and miles away. Lady Teddy was much nearer, and she was lovely and welcoming. Encouraged, he kept walking.

There were sounds in the water, like someone moving around in a bath, but Teddy couldn't see any sign of movement. It was most disconcerting, made worse by the twilight, and he kept plodding forwards and didn't find out what it was. The gloom made everything more sinister; even ordinary sounds, like a bird flapping its wings to take off from a tree, made him jump.

Ahead, there was a small strip of woodland, which was almost the only thing on his side of the river that was taller than the tall grass, and the weeds and nettles. It was time to look for shelter for the night in the wood.

It took him longer than he hoped to reach the wood because he had to leave the muddy river bank and travel into the field; it was hard to pushing his way through the long grass, and there were scuttling sounds, presumably as he disturbed small animals with his big matted paws. When he reached the woodland it disappointed him. There was no sight of a hut or shelter, and the woodland was only ten or twenty trees deep, even though it was maybe 400 metres wide. Still, it would have to do because it was getting quite dark now. He shuddered when he realised it was the sort of place that mice might like.

Teddy scanned the area, straining his eyes looking for somewhere to settle down. Then he had an idea. He would climb a tree and sleep *above* the ground. It was an excellent idea, plus he could practise climbing again, which might be useful.

It took five minutes or so to find a suitable tree, and only another five minutes to climb it, and he surprised himself by scrambling quite a good height off the ground. Some of the branches were dry and dead and Teddy managed to break some of them off and made a loose 'nest' for himself to lie on, which ended up looking something like a raft, made by a madman, up a tree. Nevertheless, Teddy was *very* pleased with his ingenuity; he was rather less please by the discomfort it caused, and it took Teddy quite a long time to fall asleep.

Then he rolled over in his sleep and fell out of the tree.

Teddy was stunned and confused for a second or two before he realised what had happened.

"Double bovver-bottoms!" he swore.

It was almost totally dark now but, more importantly, Teddy was very, very Tired. Suddenly it hit him: he might never have woken up at all if he hadn't fallen out of the tree. He decided that had no choice but to carry on, even though he was both sleepy and Tired, so with a heavy heart he decided to continue his journey ... and realised he didn't know how to get back to the river; the gloom made it impossible to see it. His immediate reaction was to run around aimlessly in the near-dark, bumping into bushes and tripping over brambles, but eventually, a spark of intelligence took over and Teddy realised that if he calmed down, and stopped making noise, he would hear the river, and could follow its sound.

He creapt through the long grass, listening carefully, adjusting his direction several times so he was always pointing at the sound of the water. The trickled grew louder, and after a few minutes he reached the river bank. Teddy wasn't sure which way to walk along the bank, but eventually remembered Ramgar had told him to follow the flow of the water, which he could just see.

As he was trudging along he thought about some of the other things Ramgar had said, remembering he had been told *not* to cross the Bredwardine Bridge at night ... but Teddy was running out of time and options. If he settled down to sleep now he risked never waking up again. He had to keep going, and he had to cross the bridge — assuming he got there before morning and hadn't fallen Asleep by then. He hoped that Clehonger wasn't too far beyond Bredwardine.

Teddy walked and walked in the summer darkness. Although there was always a faint glow in the north-western sky, it was not enough to see anything much, so Teddy was bored, but the boredom did not last long.

"Kkrrrrr!" came a sound from in front of Teddy. He couldn't tell if it was directly on the riverbank tow path, or off to one side in the long grass, or to the other side in the water. He stopped still, and gulped.

"Uh-oh," he said to himself.

Teddy stood perfectly still for many seconds. He had just decided to continue walking when he heard it again.

"Kkrrrrrrksss!"

Teddy was scared but he also knew that he had faced and come through quite a lot, and he felt something he had never felt before. He felt a little bit brave.

"Who's dare?" he shouted.

"Foxxssss...," came the slow, hissing reply, "and *you* are in my field. Either you are food, or you are challenging me."

"I am not food, and I am not challenging you. I just want to get to der bridge."

"Oh, you do, do you!" mocked the fox. "Well, I think you'll find that's not up to you, it's for me to decide."

Three days earlier, Teddy would have had no idea how to deal with this. He still wasn't certain what to do, but at least he now knew you sometimes have to stand up for yourself.

"I am going to keep walking, and you can do what you want, actchully," said Teddy.

"Err. Come on then," said Fox, obviously not expecting Teddy's response, but knowing that he couldn't back down now.

Teddy stepped forward and walked on, with his snout jutting out determinedly, until he saw Fox up-close in the gloom of the summer night. Teddy spoke first.

"Hello, I am Teddy."

"Hello," said Fox, looking like he might be regretting challenging this teddy that was twice his height.

"I am going to der Bredwardine Bridge, please step aside."

Suddenly, Fox realised that he had another line of attack and his eyes sparkled.

"So, you know about the troll under the bridge then?" he proffered, casually, with a slight smile.

"Um. No. No, I don't. Dare's a troll den?"

"Oh yes. He's quite big you know, and he hates anyone crossing his bridge. He has to listen to cars going over it all day, and it makes him very angry. So, if anyone tries to cross at night ... well, let's just say I wouldn't try it myself."

Teddy's look showed that he was trying not to be bothered.

"But of course, you are a big brave teddy, and you've nothing to worry about, have you?" glinted the Fox.

Teddy's resolve won out. "It doesn't matter. I am going to cross the bridge," yawned Teddy, trying to stay Awake. "Now, please move out of my way."

"Of course," said Fox, stepping to one side and giving him a mock bow with his head.

Teddy was unsure, but he didn't care. Either his journey would succeed, or it would fail, he was out of options now. So he reached where Fox was standing, and carried on beyond him, walking away from him, down the tow path. Fox scuttled along behind Teddy, like a grinning, toothy shadow.

"Why are you following me?" asked Teddy.

"Because this is going to be very interesting," said Fox.

Teddy's eyes opened a little wider; he really didn't want this fox following him. Quite apart from his barbed comments, Fox could probably rip Teddy apart if he put his mind to it. So Teddy started to walk faster. Fox matched his speed with ease. So Teddy sped up some more, and so did Fox. Soon Teddy and Fox were running. Teddies don't like running, and they certainly don't like running when there is a fox running after them. Teddy wondered how long he could continue to run; he was so weary, and was getting ever more Tired. The complete lack of love from this fox wasn't helping matters.

So, they ran. They ran and ran until they came to another stream joining the river. Teddy didn't break his pace and ran straight into the water. He was halfway across when he slipped on the wet stones and splashed face-down into the water. For a second he floated and was swept towards the big river, but Teddy scrambled on to his feet, fought the current and splashed through the water to the other side. He glanced over his shoulder. Fox was standing on the other side smiling. It was far from a pleasant smile; he was still mocking Teddy, but he sat down on the ground and watched Teddy run on.

Teddy was confused. Why would Fox not follow him? Maybe foxes couldn't swim? Then he remembered the story of the gingerbread man, and how the gingerbread man had ridden on the snout of a fox while the fox swam across a river. Teddy wasn't sure if that story was real or not, but the look on Fox's face was not one of frustration, it was definitely something else. He had *chosen* to stay on that side of the stream.

Still, at least Teddy was alone; it seemed better to be alone now, and for the first time in his life he found there was some enjoyment in running after all, despite being exhausted and dangerously Tired, making it all the more surprising that it was fun at all. Perhaps it wasn't surprising, however. Perhaps Teddy was simply enjoying feeling free and alive: a rebellion against the almost inevitable end to which he was rushing.

::

The advantage of running was that he covered ground more quickly. The disadvantage was that he was getting Tired at an ever-increasing rate. Even though it was very nearly dark, he was sure that he couldn't see very clearly either. He held a paw up in front of him, and it was hazy, as his running jiggled it up and down. He was sure that he had been better able to see when he was with Fox. Looking at his paw also made him realise that it was beginning to feel a bit numb from Tiredness. It was worrying.

Teddy ran though a copse that grew right up to the river, and out the other side of it, onto the open path for a short distance. Then into another copse, and again out onto the path.

All four paws were quite numb now. It was as if he was running on springs. He clapped his arm paws together, but felt almost nothing. It was weird and Teddy was getting very concerned. Now the sounds around him, and the sounds he was making, all began to take on a dullness, like he was listening to them while wearing earmuffs. This was not right. On and on he ran, but he was slowing, barely running at all; it was more like tired, uneven jog.

As he rounded a corner, he finally saw it: the fuzzy, brown shape of a bridge, some way down the river. He stopped. Unfortunately, there was another copse in front of him, but he'd found the bridge that could take him to Lady Teddy, beautifully lit by the outdoor light of an old toll house on the other side of the river.

Teddy's heart filled with excitement, and then equally quickly, he felt cold fear pouring in too. This was it. Once on the bridge, he'd see whether that silly fox has been telling the truth about the troll who supposedly lived underneath.

However, getting through the copse was not a simple matter. It turned out to be a fully-grown wood, and with Teddy's limited and fading senses he was running in darkness. As he jogged, he continually bumped into trees, spiked himself on twigs and branches and slipped over in mud. It was taking him far too long to get to the bridge. An hour later, he was still struggling to find the other side and at the point of total exhaustion.

Teddy's arms, legs and most of his body were almost totally numb; his ears were really struggling to hear at all well; he was finding it hard to think, and he was no longer sure he was even going in the right direction because he couldn't see anything at all. He was running blind. He was very, very afraid that he might actually *be* blind now. It was terrifying and frustrating. He felt so near to Lady Teddy, but he couldn't go on much longer; all he felt was his body's deepening desire to lie down, right here, and Sleep forever. It was only raw, panicked love of life that kept him moving, stumbling and clawing towards the bridge.

Teddy bumped heavily off another tree and fell over, and down a muddy bank, but he landed on something different. It was hard to tell what it was because he couldn't feel very much, but it didn't seem to be the leafy mud of the wood. Then he began to see some light. It was faint at first, but very white, even with his dull, darkened, blurred vision. It got brighter, and there was a noise: a mechanical droning sound. Suddenly Teddy realised what it was.

"AAAAAAARRRRGGGGHHHH! I'm on der road!"

The bright lights of the car, which was now nearly on top of him, showed that Teddy had fallen down an earthy bank from the wood onto the road. The car hadn't seen him and drove right at him, and there was no way he was going to move in time. He closed his eyes and waited to die. Suddenly there was the sound of screeching tyres as the car changed its course, missing him so finely that it spun him around on the spot. Teddy opened his eyes to see where the car was going. To his joy he realised he was lying no more than twenty metres from the bridge. The car drove over the bridge, and the red glow of its rear lights disappeared into the night. Eventually, it was black again. At least he knew he wasn't totally blind, yet. He struggled up and started walking towards the bridge, before he forgot which way to go.

Unfortunately, it was at this point that Teddy heard the dull, crackling sounds of a diseased voice protesting about the car. Although Teddy couldn't see, it sounded like the owner of the voice was coming towards him from the other side of the bridge. Then someone else was talking; someone whose mocking tone was vaguely familiar, and who certainly was not a friend. He would have been able to hear them both properly a few hours ago, but not now. Teddy walked a few more steps. The voices stopped and Teddy could feel someone starting to thud towards him over the bridge, and then the diseased voice rasped at him, much closer, in a loud croaking rustle that Teddy had no trouble hearing at all.

"WHAT are you doing on MY bridge?" crackled the troll, sounding massive despite his odd way of speaking, sending tiny flicks of spit even as far as Teddy's face.

"Um. Oh. I'm *on* der bridge!" began Teddy, somewhat unhelpfully. "Um. I've been trying to get to Clehonger, and I need to get to der uvver side."

"Enough! You are not going to cross!" the troll rattled. "Go back, or die. You choose. But I'm hoping you choose to die because I want to kill you."

The troll took two massive heavy footsteps towards Teddy. Each step sent vibrations through the bridge almost like someone was dropping small cars onto it. He was close now.

This was the first individual that Teddy had met who really sounded like he meant his threats. Still, what could he do? He was a nearly blind, nearly deaf teddy, with almost no feeling left in his limbs, head or body. Walking in another direction wouldn't help him for long.

He gulped and simply started to walk again. The troll took increasingly fast, heavy steps towards Teddy, gurgling and hissing and enjoying himself at this impending kill.

Teddy kept walking.

"I don't think you're going to make it over the bridge," chuckled the other voice, also now nearer and clearer. It was the voice of Fox, sitting on the bridge wall. "I cut across country to warn Troll here, in case he missed you. Goodbye, teddy bear."

Teddy stopped and gulped, just as the thundering troll reached him. It was over. Almost immediately Teddy felt the troll slam his fist up into his stomach, causing him the most immense pain he'd ever felt in his life. He flew up into the air, higher and higher. Then down, down, down and THUMP onto the bridge's parapet. It was a lucky landing, but unfortunately Teddy bounced back up into the air and, when he came down again, he slipped over the side. Teddy grasped repeatedly for the top of the parapet but in his Tired clumsiness, he snatched at it the first time and grabbed thin air instead. The results were predictable and inevitable. As if in slow motion, his paws continued to try to find something solid, even as he fell further and further away from the top of the bridge. The troll cackled with laughter as Teddy's whole body was surrounded by empty, night air. Teddy fell, faster, and faster, down towards the river. If someone were viewing it from the river bank, the whole thing would have happened very quickly, but for Teddy it took a sickeningly long time for him to hit the water. Eventually he did, with only a small splash because teddies don't weigh very much. Then the cold of the water was all around him. It felt dull to him, and he was too Tired to struggle. In any case, he could hardly make his arms or legs move. So he lay there, floating in the water, and let the water slowly soak into his stuffing, waiting for the end. As he became waterlogged, he floated lower and lower in the water. Before long he would probably sink. His mind grew darker, his vision was now totally gone. Sounds of the water in his ears became muffled and disappeared. Teddy could feel nothing. There were no sensations at all, and he couldn't think. He fell Asleep.

- Chapter 7 -

Teddy And The Dolls of Bredwardine Manor

Teddy Awoke. This was odd enough in itself, given his last memories, but particularly odd since he Awoke to a wonderful, warm feeling in the pit of his stuffing. It was gradually, very slowly, spreading to the rest of him. Although he couldn't move or see, he could just about hear muffled voices.

"His poor furry-wurry!"

"His handsome head is all grubby-wubby!"

"His body is so soggy!"

"The poor, burly teddy!"

"SERVANTS, HURRY UP!"

There was a clattering in the distance, followed by the sound of many small feet coming towards ... wherever he was.

"Finally! Now use your towels and ... things," a voice ordered. "We must clean him!"

Somehow, Teddy guessed that the owner of the voice had probably never cleaned anything in her life, much less a dirty, soggy, wet teddy. He felt many hands and brushes and small towels all over him, cleaning him and drying him, removing mud and combing fur. It was, after the past few days, a very agreeable feeling, so Teddy lay there and enjoyed it.

As they cleaned, Teddy heard the other voices still cooing over him, excited at the way that he was gradually cleaning up. Teddy liked their admiration; it made a change from vicious crocodiles, growling dogs, grumpy sheep, evil foxes and psychopathic trolls. He realised what was happening: they were not just admiring him, they were *loving* him, and that was why he was feeling warm and Awake again.

By now the warmth was flooding into all four paws and his head, and he was beginning to see. It was very blurry, but he made out some shapes. Perhaps five grey shapes close to him, who were grooming him, and several more white shapes looking on, though it was hard to see much at that distance.

"I think he is beginning to see us!"

"I think he looked at me!"

"No! He looked at me!"

"Ooooh! He's looking at *all of us*!"

This was followed by much happy squeaking and giggling.

"How odd," thought Teddy.

The immobile Teddy saw his grooms quite well now. They were small, perhaps as big as of one of Teddy's paws, and had pug-like, almost piggy faces. As he lay there, he counted them. There were at least ten of them and they were working quietly and efficiently to make Teddy look as good as any teddy had ever looked. Some were standing on the floor, all around him, and others had climbed on top of him to do what was needed to make him clean and dry.

Teddy finally saw the others who were talking. They were dolls. Perfect dolls. Perfect, extremely beautiful dolls, and they regarded Teddy as if he were their very own Prince Charming, with hands clasped under their chins and their head cocked slightly to one side. Most of these apparently artificial stereotypes of white and pink flounciness punctuated time with little statements like: "He is so burly," and "He's so handsome!" and "He's so big!" They adored him more than Teddy could understand.

Each doll was approximately the size of one of Teddy's arms, and they appeared to be made of delicate, painted china, yet somehow they were as alive as Teddy was.

Although their china faces could not make expressions, their
eyes and eyelids moved, and their mouths opened and closed and
even had some flexibility, so it was fairly easy to get some sense of
their feelings by looking at them, and the main feeling they were
showing at the moment was wide-eyed love for Teddy. It was now
definite that this was the love that had Woken him, and it was still
filling him with a deeper warmth than he'd ever felt before.

Whatever their stilted appearance, their warmth felt very real
and it had not only filled up his body, but almost completely filled
up Teddy's arms and leg paws and his head as well. Teddy could see
and hear again, and what he saw and heard was eight china dolls
looking at him and cooing.

"Hello, I'm a teddy, called Teddy!"

"Ooohh!" The Dolls giggled in unison.

"Yes, um, hello," said Teddy, unsure how to continue.

"I'm Agnes," said one of the more measured dolls. "This is
Dora, Cordelia and Bella, and this is Elspeth, Gertrude, Ffion and
Hattie," said Agnes, indicating each doll in turn.

"Pleased to meet you all!" said Teddy, with genuine gratitude.
"But can you tell me why I'm not, um, dead?"

"Oh! Oh! Dead! Oh!" said some of The Dolls to each other in
shock and alarm.

"We saved you," said Agnes, matter-of-factly.

"Really? You did?" queried Teddy, completely surprised that
these dolls could have somehow rescued him from the river and
brought him here, wherever he was.

"Yes, really," clipped Agnes.

"Well, er, okay! Thank you!" said Teddy, and Agnes'
expression softened; noticeable because she was no longer looking at
Teddy through slightly closed eyes.

"Um, where I am den?"

"You are with us, the Bredwardine Dolls. You are safe now
and you will always be safe because we will look after you, just as

Mother looks after us, and we will love you."

Teddy didn't know what to make of this. It didn't really tell him anything, except these dolls thought he was going to stay with them. Silly dolls! However, Teddy really wanted to find out how he had been rescued from the river.

"How did I get out of der river doe? I mean I remember falling and—"

"Oh that's easy! The Otters found you," droned Agnes, almost bored. "They heard a commotion on the bridge and then the next thing they knew you fell in the water and started drifting downstream. They swam over and pulled you onto our river bank, then one of them came up to the house to tell our servants."

"Oh," said Teddy, not sure what else to say.

"Then the servants and the Otters dragged you here for us to inspect. They knew we've been 'searching' for a while now, and that you might be what we were looking for, and they were right!"

Agnes was clearly much more interested in this part of the story because it involved her.

"Oh, thank you, Otters!" he said, waving out of the window, "and, um, thank you, servants!" said Teddy waving to the servants around him, with gratitude.

The servants, who were still cleaning Teddy, were startled but bowed silently where they were, and carried on cleaning.

"Funny Teddy!" laughed Agnes, and the other dolls, "Saying 'thank you' to servants indeed! Servants don't need 'thank you' you know!"

"Oh. Um, okay," said Teddy, not sure if they did or not. "Er, are you sure?"

"Of course! Look," and she asked them.

"I say, servants," shouted Agnes, smiling, "Tell this teddy here, you don't have feelings, do you?"

The servants looked at each other before one of them answered, as carefully as possible.

"We do not have feelings when we are in the presence of our mistresses, no."

It was clear to Agnes that this was merely a tactful answer, but she pretended not to understand.

"Very well then."

Most of the servants were now working together on Teddy's feet. They were scrubbing them with soapy brushes and drying them, and then repeating the process, again and again — Teddy just registered that this was happening.

"Is der sumffing wrong wiv my feet paws?" he asked.

The servants checked with The Dolls for permission to answer Teddy.

"Go on then," said Agnes, impatiently.

"Sir, it seems our abilities to remove the aromas of your journey from your feet are limited," came the response.

Teddy very slightly cocked his head on one side, trying to work out what they meant.

"Um. Do you mean I've got der smelly feets?"

The lead servant showed a hint of embarrassment but quickly regained his calm demeanour.

"I'm sure Sir has had a most trying journey, and we apologise for our shortcomings in returning your feet paws to their natural aroma. We will continue to try our best."

"Oh! I ffink I see! Don't worries cos my feets are always a bit smelly you knows!"

"You are too kind, Sir," said the lead servant, bowing.

"Indeed you are," said Agnes, smiling wryly, "Teddy, we really do have a lot to teach you about talking to servants!"

"Enough!" she barked, and waved the servants away like so many flies.

The servants took their leave of Teddy and returned to wherever they waited for their next assignment. As they left, Teddy sat up and looked at The Dolls properly, the right way up, for the first time. They were very beautiful, and they were still mostly looking at Teddy with a great deal of admiration.

Teddy leaned down and smelt his feet. He stopped sniffing almost immediately and recoiled.

"Uh-oh. Der smell of poo," said Teddy, embarrassed. The Dolls tried not to look disgusted, but didn't entirely succeed.

"Well, no matter, at least your journey is now over, and I'm sure any residual aroma will dissipate," said Agnes.

"Um. Over? Er, no, um, I'm on the way to Lady Teddy."

"Well, I'm sure you *were* but now we've rescued you, you have come to us, to be with us. You will make us ... *complete*."

The degree of matter-of-factness with which Agnes said this made it very hard for Teddy to simply tell her that she was wrong, and he'd now be on his way, thank you very much. So he said nothing and simply looked at them like a bomb had just gone off in his head.

Agnes and the other dolls glanced at each other, a little uncomfortable at this response. "Well, of course, Teddy. What did you think?"

"Um. I'm not a very clever teddy. I don't ffink I understands. Why do you want me to stay here?"

"Because you have been delivered to us to make us happy."

"I have? I fort dat I was froan off der bridge by der troll?"

"Well, yes, but it was all part of a larger fate: The Universe has brought you to us."

Teddy knew he was very small and, from what he had heard, the universe was very big, so who was he to disagree with it? However, he was finding it hard to accept that he simply had to stay here now. Quite apart from anything else, he didn't want to. He didn't know these dolls, and he didn't want to give up getting to Lady Teddy, even though it was a quest that had nearly killed him. From what Ramgar had said, Lady Teddy might be very close now. Maybe the universe was wrong, and The Dolls were wrong, and things would in fact be better if Teddy kept travelling? Teddy wasn't sure.

Agnes was watching him think, and he felt a pressure from her; from the words she had said.

Teddy had met with several individuals who had threatened him and physically tried to stop him, but these dolls clearly, genuinely loved him, or at least liked him, so they weren't threatening him like that. Nevertheless, they were also trying to stop him. With words. How could words alone stop anyone? How could they confuse him so much? This was dangerously complicated thinking for Teddy, and he wasn't used to it. Then, as if from nowhere, he had an idea. He decided to ask The Dolls if he might have tea with them. It might only delay the inevitable, but he'd get to know them a bit, and maybe he would tell them his story and they'd let him go.

"Can I have tea with you?" blurted Teddy.

The Dolls were initially surprised but, once the idea had registered, they were delighted.

"Of course! How rude of us! We must take tea together!"

Now, teddies don't need to eat or drink because their strength comes from those that love them, and since Teddy had recently been filled with love from these very unusual dolls he didn't need anything to eat or drink at all. Still, a small cup of tea had always made things better at Simon and Joanne's house, so maybe it would work here too.

"Thank you," said Teddy.

"Servants!" said Agnes.

As if by some sort of mind-reading magic, the servants immediately brought The Dolls their tea set, and they found Teddy an old china teacup and saucer; the fact that it was made from the same material as The Dolls was completely lost on him. However, unlike most dolls' tea parties, they were soon drinking real tea. While there exist some dolls and teddies that would be ruined by pouring hot tea down their insides, this was not the case at this tea party. At the time, neither Teddy nor The Dolls knew how they were able drink, but the fact is that they could and, as the servants prepared their tea, it was a moment of calm for both.

Teddy thought of a question to break the silence.

"Who is your muvver dat you mentioned den? I ffink you said she looks after you?"

"Oh. Well, she owns this house and, yes, she looks after us. We are her little girls."

"Is she a human?"

"Oh yes. Very much so, and she has taught us to be like human girls. We are very special, she found us in China. She says we do a very good job, and that we're even better than real little girls because we don't grow old, and we don't need lots of silly attention! We're here whenever she wants to admire us, and we cause her no trouble at all."

"So, um, does she love you den?"

Agnes did not respond immediately, but the other dolls adjusted their poses slightly. After a pause, Agnes answered.

"I'm certain that Mother loves us in her way, but she is an important woman, and she cannot go around being effusive! She has a position to maintain!"

"Hm, okay," mumbled Teddy. Even he could see that she was trying to convince herself.

Hattie sniffed and looked at the ceiling.

"What's der matter?"

"Oh Hattie's fine, it's nothing."

Hattie burst into tears and ran off. Agnes sighed.

Teddy thought it best not to say anything, but it was all very confusing behaviour.

One of the other dolls leaned towards Agnes and spoke in her ear. "Aggie, since we're keeping Teddy with us now, it might be acceptable to tell him about Jessica and Iona."

Agnes, opened her mouth to make a snappy return comment, paused with her mouth open, and then closed it again.

"Dora has a point." Agnes composed herself and continued, "Now, I am in *no way* criticising Mother. After all, Mother, looks after us, and gives us all the things we could ever want, but it is true that there was an incident that, hmmm, was not perhaps Mother's finest moment."

At this, there was a sound of wailing from behind the sofa, where Hattie had gone to cry.

"Gertie, dear, it's okay, go and comfort Hattie."

Gertrude wanted an assurance before leaving, "Please tell Teddy the full story, Aggie. Please."

Agnes was slightly offended at the implication, but it was overlooked because of her concern for Hattie and Gertrude, so she simply nodded and smiled an it-will-be-okay smile. Gertrude ran off to be with Hattie, and Agnes turned back to Teddy.

"Until three summers ago there were ten of us. Two of us, Jessica and Iona, who were always exploring, had climbed on to one of Mother's tables. When they made it on to the top of the table, they found a beautiful spoon, exquisitely fashioned from solid silver. They each claimed they'd found it first, and the spoon was rightfully theirs, and their disagreement became heated. They held on to different ends of the spoon, and tugged and pulled in an attempt to have it for themselves, but they didn't notice they were near the edge of the table."

Agnes, swallowed, her eyes full of sadness.

"They both fell off the table, and they broke. They died immediately. It was horrible, but at least it was quick."

At this point, both Hattie and Gertrude wailed from the other side of the room, and broke down in sobs, and several of the other dolls now had tears in their eyes too.

"So, I went to tell Mother. Now, in some ways what happened next was my fault, Mother was working and I interrupted her.

However, her response was not what I expected. She just came into our room ..." Agnes was clearly having great difficulty continuing. "She ..." Agnes cleared her throat, " ... she, well, she picked up Iona and Jessica, muttered, 'useless!', and threw them in the bin and left."

Teddy couldn't believe it. Their 'mother' had simply found no further use for two broken dolls and had thrown them away without a second thought.

"But she's your mother, and you're like her daughters! Dat's terrible."

"I said, quite clearly, that it was not Mother's finest moment, but I also said it was not my place to criticise her. Nor is it yours."

Agnes' mouth was firm and pursed, and she stared at Teddy with a gaze that made it clear that this point was not negotiable.

"I'm not a very clever teddy, and I don't know some of der words you said, but I'm confused. Does she loves you or not?"

Agnes, seemed to want to say something but couldn't quite get the words right. Dora looked at her, as if to say, 'go on, tell him', so Agnes did.

"It is something that we have trouble with too."

Her gaze dropped and, for the first time Agnes looked less than totally in control. Dora spoke.

"We believe it is why you have come to us. We are dolls, we have to love properly or we have no purpose. We love to be adored and admired, and we love in return. We *have* to love. We have heard stories of other dolls, elsewhere, out there, that are owned by little human girls who comb their doll's hair, and dress them, and play with them. It would be so easy to love such an owner, or anyone who could genuinely love us and appreciate our beauty, but since Jessica and Iona's accident we have all, to a greater or less extent, had great trouble loving Mother ..."

Agnes raised her hand to indicate a point of order, and was going to speak when Dora anticipated her and continued.

" ... although we do very, very much value Mother's protection and provision for us. We are obviously richer than most; that is clear to us, and to anyone else who looks out of that window at those who toil below. Nevertheless, we do have trouble loving Mother, and it eats away at us, and that is why we are overjoyed that you are here with us now, because we have no trouble loving you, and you yourself seem to need to be loved."

Teddy couldn't work out what to say. It was confusing how their Mother could be so generous and yet so lacking in feelings. He found himself asking out loud, for the third time:

"So you finds it hard to loves your muvver, but does your muvver love *you*?"

Again, Hattie and Gertrude wailed from behind the chair, and two of the other dolls, also began to sob.

"Oh. Sorry. Didn't mean to—"

"It's okay, Teddy," said Agnes. "It is a valid question, and here is my answer: I would like to believe she does, in her own way, but I know others find it hard to accept." Agnes, gestured towards the tears.

"Hm. Does you *trusts* your muvver den? Um. If dis doll ..." Teddy pointed at one of them, and made an expression as if to ask, 'what's your name?'

"Bella," replied Bella shyly, with a hint of a smile.

" ... if Bella got a bit broked, would you tell your muvver?

Bella's eyes opened wide with fear. The prospect of being damaged, and less-than-perfect, was terrifying.

"Would you mind if she was taken away by your muvver?" asked Teddy.

Another doll replied almost instantly.

"Yes! Yes, we would mind a lot!" She was clearly upset by the suggestion, and took Bella's hand.

"Elspeth is right," added Agnes. "It is true. If she wasn't dead, I think we would all make sure Mother did not find out. We would have to make up some excuse for Bella not being around but we would get the servants to fix her, as well as possible, and we would look after her. She is one of us."

Another doll, perhaps the most beautiful of the group, tutted and sighed.

"Yes, Cordelia, we *would* look after her, even if she were no longer perfect, and we would do the same for you."

Cordelia was immediately appalled at the prospect of being anything other than utterly wonderful.

"We are aware of our frailty, and we are aware of our needs," continued Agnes. "We need someone to love, someone who will make us feel special, appreciated and safe. We need to love ... *you*."

She gazed openly at Teddy with eyes that showed her feelings for him, and her fear of rejection. Teddy again spoke without thinking.

"I'm a bit confused now. I mean, you're all really nice, and very pretty, and if I could I'd stay here ..." The Dolls again clasped their hand together under their chins and made happy 'Ooh!' noises, " ... but I don't know what to do, cos I've got dis ffingy I got to do. I got to find Lady Teddy. I ffink. Hm. Dis is confusing."

Agnes did not react with anger, she had a better, more honest idea. She walked up to Teddy, put her delicate hands on his chest, looked up into his eyes and whispered softly, so only Teddy could hear her. It was a simple plea.

"Please, forget everything else. Just hold me in your arms, and make me feel safe to be made of china."

How could he resist? He bent down and held her in his arms. The warmth in the middle of his stuffing glowed hot as he did it. No one had ever loved him like this, but when Teddy stopped hugging, the feeling dissipated surprisingly quickly, and it left him feeling strangely empty.

"You will stay with us, Teddy," stated Agnes gently, "because we need you here."

"But, I'm not sure! Can't I choose what I want?"

"No, and why would you want to? Out there is danger and fear and uncertainty. You have been out there and it nearly killed you. You cannot choose because you make the wrong choices. We will choose for you, and we will give you purpose, and you will be safe and loved."

All this seemed very logical. But Teddy still felt, in his stuffing, that something was wrong with all this, and it panicked him.

"So it doesn't matter what I want den?"

"Well, hm, obviously it matters a bit. We're not terrible you know. We love you! Moreover, you have not been very good at deciding your path, so we will now do it for you. It makes sense, and it's good for all of us. Surely you can see that?"

"Um. I suppose so."

"There, then it's settled."

"Er, no, no. I didn't say dat!"

"But why? My argument is clear, and we will all benefit. What else is there to say?"

Teddy thought and thought, and while he was thinking he noticed that the warmth in his middle was not as warm as it had been. He also noticed that the face of The Dolls were not as enamoured as they had been because he was questioning whether he should stay.

To some extent they were right, it would be good for everyone if he stayed. Maybe what he wanted didn't matter? Maybe what he wanted was wrong? It was entirely possible, he usually wasn't very good at working out what to do, but something still waved madly in his mind, telling him not to give in. Telling him staying here, like this, was not right.

"It's not right! I ffink I can choose what I do! Sometimes I do der wrong ffingies, and sometimes I do the right ffingies, but I can choose, I ffink."

"No, you can't. We won't let you, and it's for your own good. In fact, if you try to leave we will stop you. Obviously, we are in control around here," stated Agnes, calmly gesturing out of the window again at the world beyond. "If we want you to stay here, then you will stay. If you leave, you will find that you don't get far before being brought back. It's not just servants and otters that listen to us. There are dogs, and birds of prey, and there are horses and other farm animals, and all of them owe us a debt and listen to us and will do what we ask. You will not get far."

The warmth from the hug a few seconds earlier was barely perceptible now.

"But this is not how we want it to be. We would like you to *want* to be here. We do not think it is a lot to ask. After all, we saved your life."

Teddy gulped because they'd done more than that; they had *given* him life, or at least fanned it into flame. He felt rather ungrateful. Yet, still something was telling him he was being moved around like a piece of furniture. It was obvious that they were better thinkers than him, and he could never hope to argue his way out of this. It was also clear, if they truly were as powerful as Agnes had said, that he could never hope to escape without their blessing. He was trapped, and he hated feeling trapped.

That was it.

"Do you care dat I feel trapped?"

"Of course, but it will pass."

"Simon says dat love means you want to makes der ovver person happy; dat's what he told me once, and I rememerized it cos it sounded importants."

"I don't know who Simon is, but I'm not at all sure that I agree with him."

"So what do you ffink dat love is den?"

Teddy's tummy now only felt the barest glimmer of love from The Dolls.

"Giving someone what they need, whether they like it or not, because that's the best thing for them."

"But isn't dat what your muvver does for you, doe? And you don't ffink your muvver loves you really very much, you said."

Agnes' mouth fell open. Some of the other dolls looked at each other with surprise at this highly potent attack.

Dora spoke. "Teddy. You are not as silly as you think. You are making us question our decision, but you are also making us question our feelings. I'd be careful, if I were you."

"I know. I can feel you are not so warm towards me now."

"You can?"

Teddy nodded, which perhaps shook the stuffing enough in his head to give him a simple, silly idea, and as usual it came pouring out of his mouth.

"Can't you love each other?"

Elspeth squeaked, and Bella quickly looked away, embarrassed. Agnes pretended not to notice.

"What do you mean?"

"Well, maybe I'm a silly teddy, but I ffink you said you need to love someone?"

"Yes."

"So why can't you love each other?"

"Because ... It's not that simple, you see. That is, we ..."

"We have never thought about it," said Dora, calmly.

"We have not," agreed Agnes.

For a few seconds, no one spoke. Teddy continued.

"Also, I ffink dat you knows lots of folk already, cos you said dat you control lots of dem; don't you love any of dem?"

This time Ffion squeaked. It was all the more shocking because she had said nothing at all to this point, and was by far the most quiet and demure of The Dolls. Agnes noticed and seemed to be making a mental note to talk to Ffion later, then she continued.

"No, we do not love these others that you mention, we need

someone else to love, but someone who is *meant* to be an object of our love. You are still our hope."

Teddy felt a lone spark of warmth flicker inside him, as she stared at him.

"But, but, hm, wouldn't it be better to find someone who loves you already, and wants to be wiv you because day choose it?"

"Of course, but that's not how things are."

"I ffink it is doe. I ffink you like each uvver, and you'd miss each uvver if you get broken, and you've said so."

Agnes couldn't help but see Teddy's point, even though Teddy was bumbling around the World of Thought like a bull in a china shop trying to make a cup of tea.

"Maybe you could luvs uvvers too, if you let yourselves? Wivout forcing dems? Maybe dat would be better?"

"But what if we loved someone and they didn't love us back? If we didn't make them love us, then we would be hurt. Maybe some of us have felt that hurt before and don't want to feel it again."

Despite her words, Agnes was beginning to see the flaw in her argument.

"Do you makes your friends luvs you den?" said Teddy opening his arm paws to include all The Dolls around the room.

"No. Of course not" said Agnes, looking at the ground. "But what can we do? We really do need you. Dolls need someone *else*."

"You all look like der someone elses to me!" laughed Teddy, in his roly-poly way. "You are all friends, and you like each uvver and I ffink you could love each uvver and make each uvver feel special, and I ffink you could love uvvers dat you knows already. I don't ffink you needs me here at all, doe I do ffink you are all very pretty and clever, but I ffink I needs to go and find Lady Teddy because I have come so far dat I can't stop now. I can't let her go, and never find out if she loves me. And I ffink dat if you don't let me go den you are like your muvver who just *looks at you*, like … garden gnomes. Dat's what I ffink."

This outburst of Teddy's was too much for many of The Dolls, more than half of them now openly wept. Bella and Elspeth held each other and sobbed together. Ffion wept quietly, all the while looking over to where the servants would be waiting to come out at a moment's notice. Cordelia merely looked confused then picked up a mirror to check her hair. Gertrude and Hattie walked from the sofa to the others, supporting each other as they cried, even Dora took Agnes' hand and smiled, supportively.

"What if we did let you go?" enquired Agnes. "Would you do it? Would you leave us?"

"I ffink I would go, but some of me would like to stay here. Because you are very lovely." Teddy found himself looking into Agnes' eyes when he said this, and felt shy, and continued. "I mean, you're all lovelies, but I ffink I would go. Den maybe I could come back to see you sometime? I'd like to."

"And you would go to live with this 'Lady Teddy', even though you have never spoken to her?"

"I ffink I *have* to. I have to know if she likes me, because she's a teddy and I'm a teddy and she looked like she wanted me, and dat's what I really need, just like you really need someone to love. And maybe if der teddies and der dolls all find love for each uvver den dat's good?"

Agnes sighed, emotion showing in her eyes too. It was clear Teddy would never willingly admire and appreciate them if she made him stay.

"Very well, maybe you're right. Maybe I am acting like Mother. Hm. I know that's not an entirely good thing." She looked out of the window for a moment and made her mind up. "We do, in our way, love you. It would be ... *good*, if you came back sometime."

"You mean I can go?"

Agnes looked around, no one seemed to object. She turned away to stare out of the window, to think, mulling over her options, then turned back to Teddy.

"Look, if you go, it will not be easy for you. You will have to travel through Moccas. We are in conflict with Moccas. Actually, everyone is in conflict with Moccas because recently they have become intolerable. But I'm certain you would not be safe there if they knew you had come from us. In any case, they seem to attack almost everyone on sight. How far do you need to go beyond their lands?"

"I'm not sure. All I know is I need to get to Clehonger."

"Ah. It is safe there, though it is quite a long way to walk, even for a burly teddy with big legs!" Agnes smiled a resigned smile despite her crestfallen stance.

"How long do you think it would take me?"

"A day? Maybe a little more. It's hard to tell. Few in these parts travel that far, except for humans of course. They go *everywhere* in their cars. But I *suppose* we could find out how you'd get there ... if you like."

"I ffink," began Teddy, "dat I like it a lot less dan I did, but I ffink I still have to do it."

Agnes closed her eyes for a moment, and then opened them again. She had lost him.

"Very well. You can go. I'm *letting* you go." Her eyes were welling up with tears now. Teddy poddled over to her, bent down and gently hugged her again, and let her cry a little on his fur. After a while she composed herself and stood up.

"Servants!" she called, her voice cracking with emotion.

Servants scattered into the room and ran over to The Dolls.

"Our plans have changed. Explain to this teddy how to get to Clehonger. Then show him the way to the road. That is all."

She turned away from them.

For a moment the servants waited, then realised that they really should go, right now. So they did, and Teddy went with them, feeling like he'd just done something cruel.

Twenty minutes later Teddy was standing at the wrought iron

gates at the front of Bredwardine Manor House, after being
provided with everything he needed by the servants. He looked up
at the large middle window on the second floor where The Dolls
were, and waved sadly. His tummy felt pangs of sadness. Then he
turned round and walked up the lane, out of sight, toward Moccas.

- Chapter 8 -

Teddy And The Moccasins of Moccas

Teddy had a map. It was his first map ever, and he still wasn't sure he understood how to use it. He remembered being told that the blue square was The Dolls' manor house and the green cross was Clehonger, and the wiggly black line between them was the road along which he was walking. He had noticed that the road at his feet wasn't actually black, it was more of a grey colour, and he hoped that didn't matter. There were some other marks on the map, including a red blob that Teddy remembered was something to do with Moccas, and he noticed that the black road line went through the red blob. However, the thing he focused on was that he was going to walk along this road from one end of the wiggly black line to the other, and nothing was going to stop him this time.

After walking for less than half an hour, Teddy began to hear strange noises. Flapping sounds and an odd noise, something like the sound a toddler might make if it tried to say, "Mee."

A car drove by, and as with many of the other cars that had passed him, it suddenly started driving a little erratically after seeing Teddy walking along. Teddy quickly pressed himself into the hedge in the hope that he'd disappear and they'd convince themselves that they'd been seeing things. After the car's noise had faded, Teddy continued walking and noticed that the flapping and toddler sounds had also gone. Then they started again. A few seconds later something jumped out from under hedge. It was a very strange creature, something like a slipper, but whereas a slipper simply goes on your foot, this one was flapping over the ground on its own. Teddy remembered the servants telling him about odd flappy creatures called Moccasins and guessed that this was one of them. If that was so then Teddy was now in the region of Moccas.

"Ah! Fluffy! Walky forward. Very fluffy. Odd. Danger?" said the Moccasin. Then it flapped back into the roadside hedge.

Teddy stopped and looked around, and wondered if that really had just happened. He waited, but the odd creature didn't return. Teddy shook his head and carried on walking.

It was a beautiful day, if a little too hot for Teddy because of his fur. Still, it was otherwise undeniably perfect, with an iridescent blue sky and one or two fluffy clouds, which Teddy thought looked like sheep. The gorgeous warm sun heated the trees and grass and bushes so that they made a wonderful summery country smell. Then three Moccasins flopped out of the bush onto the road.

"Yes. Fluffy. Walky. Walky. Bad? Stop?" said one.

This might have been a question because the next Moccasin seemed to answer.

"OH! Bad, maybe. Yes. Bad, maybe. Get help!"

The third Moccasin was a little bit better at talking.

"Dangerous invader! HUFF? Smelly feet! Smelly feet! Warn!"

They too disappeared into the hedge. Teddy didn't know what to do, if anything, but it sounded like they thought he was a threat. He decided they were silly and carried on walking towards Clehonger.

Sheep were grazing and baa-ing in the field opposite under some large oak trees, bees buzzed: it all made for a lovely walk, apart from the weird creatures that kept popping out. He wondered if the Moccasins would return.

Two minutes later he found out. As he passed a gate, a horde of Moccasins ambushed him, surrounding him in seconds while screaming as loudly as they could. More flapped from under the gate and jumped from the top of the hedge, and wiggled from underneath it. They were on his head, and flapping at his feet, and there was no escape. They tripped him and toppled him over. They flapped in his face and they jumped on top of him. It hurt. Even though Teddy's fur and stuffing was a natural protection in most places on his body, their attack was so violent, so numerous, and so overwhelming that they were bound to hurt him some of the time, even if it was just by accident.

Stunned by the surprise and the repeated slappings, Teddy tried to push them off him, and shouted that they were hurting him, and asked them what he'd done to deserve this. He struck out with his feet trying to kick some of them away from him, but without success, until he accidentally caught his foot inside one of the Moccasins and it ended up on Teddy's foot like a shoe. It immediately stopped moving. The others froze.

"Murderer! Murderer!" they shouted, over and over again, as they backed away in fear. Then they flapped away as if their lives depended on it. Almost as soon as they had attacked, they were gone and the attack was over.

"Dat," said Teddy to himself, "was weird."

However, the inanimate Moccasin still lay on the ground. Teddy walked up to it and peered at it. It was a piece of footwear. He nudged it with his foot paw, but there was no life in it at all. It seemed they were right; it was dead; he really had killed the poor thing. Teddy swallowed. He hadn't meant to do it any harm, he had just wanted them to stop hurting him.

He stared at it for well over a minute wondering if there was anything he could do, and decided that there wasn't. Indeed, he imagined that even if he could have revived the Mocassin, it would probably thank him by trying to slap him in the face or by jumping up and down on his head. It was sad but there was nothing to be done, he would have to move on.

Teddy resumed his walk again. Step after step along the road, on his way towards his Lady Teddy. He glanced back at the now tiny shape of the lifeless Moccasin in the distance, and then kept walking. The day didn't seem so beautiful now.

Less than one minute later, it happened again. This time five Moccasins jumped out in front of him.

"You very mad teddy! You potty-bonkers, silly teddy. With mad on top of d'mad!" shrieked one of the Moccasins. His voice sounded like a human who had been breathing helium for more than a minute, and was not only high-pitched but was also oxygen-deprived and seriously disoriented.

"You come with us. Or you die! Die, die, die! Or come with us. Choose now please. Thanking you!" said another Moccasin.

The other three flip-flopped behind Teddy and tried to shepherd him off the road and into the field next to it. It was unlikely to work because Teddy was at least twenty times their height, and fifty times their weight. Not surprisingly, they were totally ineffectual.

"What are you *doing*?" asked Teddy.

"Helping. Helping quickly. Helping now. Or die! Please? Thank you!" said the second Moccasin.

Their urgency was different from that of the other Moccasins. They seemed concerned for Teddy's safety, and for their own safety too. Since they scanned left and right nervously as they spoke, it seemed it wasn't Teddy who scared them.

The five Moccasins were different colours. The first Moccasin was black, the second brown, two of the three that had wheeled round behind him were beige (and muddy) and the last was a very dark blue. Teddy watched them trying in vain to move him off the road, until they seemed to give up.

"Okay, you die. Bye!" said Black, and the Moccasins began to leave.

"No! Wait! Why duz you want me to come wiv you den?"

"Can't talk now. Get off road fast. Very fast. Talk elsewhere," added Brown.

"Hm, well, okay, maybe I come wiv you a little way."

"Good. Big teddy, you come now. Thank you!" said Black, the leader, happily.

So Teddy followed them. They hadn't attacked him and they did seem concerned for his safety. This was a distinct improvement compared to the others he had met. Teddy's only concern was that he was now leaving the road and therefore leaving the route on his map, but he would have to sort that out later.

The field, on the other side of the gate, was at the bottom of a small hill, which they now climbed. As they did, it became progressively more wooded. If these Moccasins were genuinely trying to take Teddy to safety, then it would give them some visual shelter from the other, more vicious Moccasins; if not then no one would ever see whatever it was that they had planned for Teddy. They arrived at a particularly big tree.

"You hide behind tree. You very big! Need big tree! Funny, big teddy!"

Teddy did as they asked, and sat down. The five gathered around him and Black spoke.

"How you not dead already! You walk by Park of Moccas! Where Masters live! Masters! You should be dead! Very dead!"

"Huh?" said Teddy.

Brown joined in, "Teddy very silly, very slow. We cleverest. Explain to simple teddy." Brown flapped from side to side as he spoke. "We fight for other Moccasins. Freedom from the Masters! We 'The Five'," he declared, proudly.

"Park of Moccas. Down there. Where *army* of Moccasins lives!" added Blue, with awe in his voice, turning to look down the hill at the park on the other side of the road.

"Masters live there, in The Wood. Beyond park. Masters very bitter. Very angry with The Dolls. With everyone!" added Brown.

"Der Dolls! I know dem! Why are der Masters angry wiv der Dolls?" Teddy was concerned, and felt protection rising in him like a panic.

"Yes, we explaining. Dolls. Snooty dolls. Think they so strong. Think they tell everyone what to do. Moccasins don't like snooty dolls. Moccasins want to do what Moccasins want. Masters help us!" continued Brown.

"But then Masters not good. Masters go bad. We think badder than dolls. Other Moccasins not agree with us. Other Moccasins want kill dolls. Want kill teddy! Happy do what Masters say. But teddy done nothing. We help the teddy," explained Black. "We think and plan. Then we do. Five save Moccasins from Masters! The Five save the *teddy* from Masters!"

"Ffank you!" said Teddy, beginning to believe that these five pieces of demented footwear were trying to help him.

"Teddy has smelly feet!" shouted one of the Beige twins. "I smells them!"

The Moccasins drew back away in fear.

"Oh, yes, I stepped in der poo, and I can't get rid of der smell," admitted Teddy, embarrassed.

The Five stopped backing away, but were clearly very unsettled.

"Sorry, it's bad isn't it?" worried Teddy, noting their reaction.

"Hm. Masters speak of HUFF. HUFF coming to destroy Moccasins. You are HUFF? Or not? Tell," said Black, sounding concerned.

"Um, what's a 'huff'? One of der uvver Moccasins said dat too I ffink."

"Not *a* HUFF. Just HUFF. Herald. Herald of United Foul-Feets. Foul-footed humans unite and kill us. Put their feet in us and kill us. Herald comes first. Herald has smelly feet. Herald comes *just before* humans kill us. All us."

Teddy had learned enough from his travels that he didn't think it would be a good idea to tell them about the dead Moccasin, and how his foot had killed him.

"Dat's *awful*," he said, with complete honesty.

"It is. Here we are free. There not free." Black turned to look down the hill and over the road to the large park. "In the Park of Moccas. Masters rule. But we make Moccas free. Flapping and free. Masters make us *not* free. Dolls make us *not* free. Masters want us attack dolls. So, you HUFF?"

"Er, I don't ffink so. I'm Teddy. Dat's me!" Teddy laughed a nervous roly-poly laugh. "Just got smelly feet, dat's all."

The Five seemed to believe Teddy and their agitated flapping gradually subsided. There was an awkward silence as they stared at Teddy, still unsure of him, and he looked back, with no idea what to say to them. Suddenly Brown started to flap around like there was a fire underneath him.

"Ooh! Idea! Others not know Teddy not HUFF. Can scare them? Maybe. Help us? Maybe?" Brown looked at Black to see what he thought.

"Like idea! Planning time. Come!" Black led the way and they all flapped far enough that Teddy couldn't hear them talk.

Teddy didn't mind. It meant that he could sit and enjoy the warm summer breeze in the shade of this tree and look at the beautiful view of this troubled land.

After a few minutes, however, Teddy's mind began to wander. Maybe he should leave now? Perhaps he should travel through the fields until he was out of Moccas, and then work his way down to the road? At least he was on the safer side of the road here, away from the park. The problem was that he knew he would get lost. He needed to get down to the road fairly quickly, while he remembered how to do it; otherwise he'd lose his way and need to ask someone — and his journey had taught him not to take that kind of risk.

Before he decided what to do, The Five returned.

"Have plan! You help? Plan is good. We 'capture' you. We capture the 'HUFF'. Show others we strong, we clever. Clever Five. Clever planners. Show we better than the Masters. Others follow us. Masters no longer masters. Us happy. You help with plan? Help, yes?" Black sounded hopeful, but concerned that Teddy might say no.

Teddy had learned a lot over the last few days because, instead of saying 'yes' or 'no' with a happy chuckle, he actually tried to think about the plan. It wasn't just his own safety that he considered. He was also concerned that the Masters might be planning to do something bad to The Dolls. Something inside him ached when he thought about them being hurt. Perhaps, if the Five's plan worked, it would be a way to keep The Dolls safe from the Masters' anger? Why were they bitter and angry? What might they do to The Dolls? Deep in his stuffing, Teddy knew he had to do what he could to help The Dolls.

"Okay den, I'll help."

The Five were ecstatic, shouting 'Happy!' and squeaking.

"Happy! Happy! Can return to The Park! Can be with others! Thank you!"

"S'okay. I likes to help!" said Teddy, and unusually for him, he didn't tell them why.

"You very good teddy. We like!" said Blue.

Teddy felt a little guilty, but he didn't have time to dwell on it because at that moment Black launched into a description of what would happen, and how they would use Teddy to get to the Masters.

Afterwards, Black ordered them to break camp and, without further thought, they descended toward the Park of Moccas.

It was only as they were nearing the road that Teddy began to realise that there were aspects of this plan that he hadn't thought through. It was possible that this plan might help The Dolls by stopping the Masters, but what would happen then? Could he walk away? What if he really was the HUFF somehow? After all, he had killed a Moccasin with his foot. He didn't *feel* like the HUFF but—

"Invaders! Renegades! You stop! You stop now!"

It was a group of nine or ten Moccasin guards. They had burst out from behind the gate and blocked the gateway to the road. The Five now put their plan into action. This was when they would find out if it worked or not. Black began:

"Captured the HUFF! You look! HUFF is big and fluffy! Has smelly feet!"

The guards recoiled. It was true, this did look and smell a lot like the HUFF, as described by the Masters, but amazingly he seemed to be under control of these renegades. Black spoke again.

"You come with us. You join us. We stronger than the Masters. We stronger than the HUFF. We cleverer. You join us!"

Some of the guards gasped at this kind of talk. If the Masters knew, they would do very horrible things, probably to everyone now gathered around this gate.

"Masters have made us strong! Masters are strong. How you stronger? We not want hurt by Masters," said the lead guard, standing in front of the others.

"Masters are worse than dolls. Masters hurt us. Masters have not got HUFF. *WE* have got HUFF. We strong. HUFF not hurt you. You safe, if you with us," countered Black.

The guards considered the argument. It was true that the Masters had hurt a number of them, and this did look and smell like the HUFF, and it really did seem these Five had captured him and had him under control. They looked at each other, but before they could deliberate any further, Black stepped in.

"No. You choose now. You with us? You against? If you against, you die. We let the HUFF kill you. You choose now!"

Teddy didn't like the sound of this. He did *not* intend to kill anyone. Killing was bad enough as an accident, he certainly did not want to kill on purpose. Before he could object, the threat worked.

"We join you! You not release the HUFF! We join!"

"Good," said Black. "Good choice. We all Moccasins. We decide what we do. We not need Masters."

There was some tension in the air, but the guards joined

ranks with the Five quickly enough, and together they flapped under the gate, and onto the road, while Teddy slowly climbed over. Then they all crossed the road to the other side, and under or over another gate into the Park.

The further into The Park that they walked, the more frequently they met other groups of Moccasins, some gambolling in the field, others guarding an entrance or a point of strength on the landscape. Each time they met someone, Black used the same call to action, and each time it got easier to persuade them, due to their increasing numbers.

By the time they reached the edge of the Moccas Wood, there were more than 200 in the group. Teddy was increasingly nervous, because all but five of them probably wanted to kill him. He wasn't at all sure that the Five would be able to retain control and, if all these Moccasins did attack him, they would easily overcome him and start hurting him; it might take a long time but eventually he would die.

"YOU STOP!" shouted the leader of a group of guards on the edge of the Wood — it was clearly terrified that it and its compatriots had the job of stopping several hundred other Moccasins from entering Moccas Wood.

"Will not!" answered Black loudly, but calmly. "We will see the Masters. Their time is over. We are all Moccasins. This is our park. We will be free. We have captured the HUFF. You come with us or you die!"

Black didn't need to threaten to release Teddy any longer. The several hundred twitchy Moccasins behind him were a genuinely much greater threat. The guards saw they were supporting a lost cause, and yielded almost immediately.

However, behind them someone was not quite as compliant. A brown Moccasin flapped off into the wood as fast as possible, presumably to tell the Masters what was happening.

"Get him!" shouted Black. Several fast-running Moccasins

dashed forwards and rushed after the would-be messenger. They were much faster and soon jumped on top of him, all flapping madly, making leaves and dust puff around them. The messenger was dead in seconds.

Teddy gulped. This was not what he wanted, not at all: he was going to enter a dark wood with several hundred murderous Moccasins.

They moved on, into Moccas Wood, forcing their way through sentry posts and brutally overcoming any resistance. Teddy wished he could get away but couldn't think of a way to leave without causing more mayhem and death, probably including his own death.

As they approached the middle of the wood, the trees began to open out into a sunny glade, and in the middle of glade was a large group of Moccasins, gathered around six assorted figures. The most obvious creature, in the centre, was a large Blacksheep, like those Teddy had seen at Ramgar's Circle. On her back, seated on a small saddle, was a tiny figure that, even from this distance, struck Teddy as being rather like one of the doll's servants. To his left were two foxes, standing side-by-side. To his right were an otter and a mole. Even the mole was taller than the tallest Moccasin. These were The Masters. Mole spoke first, with a particularly sickly smile on his face.

"We're not stupid you know. We have been watching you. You over-grounders never see my spies. You can't reach us underground. We..." (he indicated the six Masters) "...have been waiting for you."

"Indeed we have," said a small, calm, smooth voice from the back of the Blacksheep. "Would-be attackers, I regret to inform you that you will fail in your attempt to overcome us. I'm sure it is most regrettable to you, but we will prevail."

Teddy heard worried chattering from behind him. The calm, smooth voice continued. "I see you have brought the HUFF with you. How kind."

Turning to his Moccasin followers he continued, "You see, the

HUFF arrives, as we said he would. Now is the time that you need us the *most*, to protect you from his evil threat. These are *dark* times when renegades among you join forces with the HUFF to attack you, and all so that the united humans can pour down upon to wipe you out, but I know we will stand strong, side-by-side, and with our help, *you will overcome!* You will overcome the HUFF, *and* the humans, *and* The Dolls!"

At this, the circle of supporters, which was at least as large in number as the group behind Teddy, roared with support. The foxes smiled toothy smiles, and the otter repeatedly stood up and sat down on its hind legs, too excited to sit still; the mole monitored the situation carefully, and the Blacksheep stood firm and immovable in the centre, expressionless.

Teddy felt very, very worried indeed. He was completely surrounded by lunatics. Worse, it was certain that some of those *behind* him had been swayed by the Masters' speeches. "Dis is very not good," he thought.

Before Teddy could think himself deeper into worry, however, the foxes parted. One moved to the left of the central group, and the other stayed on the right. This looked a lot like the beginning of a strategy being put into action.

As the foxes moved, every member of the Moccasins in the glade turned to face their enemies, but Black was not going to wait to be wiped out.

"They lie! It is *they* who enslave us. We have *captured* HUFF. We are strong! ATTACK!"

It worked well enough. A large number of the Moccasins surged around Teddy towards the Masters' group, pouring around Teddy's feet, like he was standing in a stream. Teddy didn't know what to do, so he stood still and tried to think.

The foxes took charge of the counter-attack, sending curtains of Moccasins left and right to contain the forces of the Five, while the main force made a frontal attack. It was enough to confuse some of the Five's forces, and the carnage began. Before long Teddy saw many motionless Moccasins lying static in various positions, all dead. The foxes were safe behind a barrier of their Moccasins, but the Five were becoming increasingly at risk as their Moccasin force became fragmented. Teddy needed to do something to stop the slaughter but he was distracted by a group of Moccasins that were flapping at his feet, trying to hurt him. They were mostly ineffectual because there were so few focused on Teddy, but occasionally they stung him quite badly. If a larger number started to attack him, or if he fell over, then his worst fears would be realised. He really had to do something now. If only he could think quicker.

Then he had an idea.

"WAIT!" he shouted immediately. Almost no one heard him above the noise.

"W A I T !" he bellowed, louder than he'd ever shouted before. Only a few Moccasins stopped to look.

"HUFF WANTS SOME NEW SLIPPERS!" bellowed Teddy, desperate about the danger growing all around him.

Those attacking Teddy stopped immediately and drew back, and many nearby stopped fighting and gaped at him in fear. Others checked to see why it had gone quiet near the HUFF, and soon everyone was still, looking at Teddy, waiting for him to speak.

"Dat's better. I must tell you sumffing," Teddy said, solemnly.

At this, the Masters became nervous. The servant Master on the Blacksheep was going to talk, but Teddy would not let him.

"No. I *will* tell you sumffing," he repeated, firmly. "I am NOT the HUFF. I am a teddy, called Teddy, and I'm travelling to Clehonger, and dat's all. Dare's no need for you to fight each other because you are all der Moccasins, and I'm your friend."

As he spoke, the two forces quickly began to use the opportunity to re-group. Both sides had taken many casualties. Perhaps a fifth of all the Moccasins already lay dead on the ground, revealed as the groups returned to their original positions.

"How interesting!" said the Servant Master. "He has no idea who he is! In fact, you *are* the HUFF! I know for certain because I *invented* you!"

The Blacksheep smiled; the first expression she had shown since Teddy had arrived. Teddy's mind raced as fast as it could. What did the Servant Master mean? Teddy noticed that some the Masters were whispering to each other about this point too, and the mole, in particular, had a very concerned expression. However, to Teddy it was simple.

"How could you invent me? I'm me! I'm Teddy!"

"Without a doubt you are a teddy, but you are also the HUFF. I heard about you days ago. For various reasons, I have spies in Llandegley. They told me you were dirty and smelly, and that your journey would lead you to Clehonger. I knew you would come this way. So, I quickly 'warned' these good Moccasins about you."

"But I'm not a Harold of anyffing."

"Herald."

"Hair-ald ... but I'm not der HUFF."

"Oh but the wonderful thing is that you *are*, even if you don't know it. You're more than a teddy, you're a symbol, with meaning, and you've arrived here exactly as I predicted. You confirm that I am right, and that I am a wise leader. By the time I'm finished, you may even *choose* to help me, I may conquer you and make the HUFF serve the good Moccasins of Moccas! So, Teddy, my HUFF, come here and talk to me and fulfil your *destiny!*"

The Servant Master had stoked the crowd well and a massive cheer went up from the Moccasins, including many behind Teddy.

Black whispered to Teddy, with a tone of emergency.

"Don't listen. He try to use you. He take you from me. My group collapse!"

Teddy managed to see what was happening. If the Servant Master took him away from the Five, their group would no longer have the HUFF, they would have no rallying point, and they would be easily destroyed. Teddy couldn't think further than that, but it was enough.

"No. You come here, to me, alone." Teddy was firm.

Everyone was surprised, not least Black. The Servant Master might come to *them*. The Masters moved together to talk. A few moments later the Servant Master spoke.

"For the sake of my people, I will risk my life and come over to you with BlackMaa here. I do not walk well since an accident, so she must carry me."

"Okay den. Come here," agreed Teddy.

BlackMaa started to trot slowly through the ranks of Moccasins, then over the dead Moccasins, and then through the Moccasins of The Five. BlackMaa stopped in front of Teddy, no more than a few centimetres away, The Servant Master on her back looking down at him.

"What do you want, Teddy? What does my *invention* want?"

"I am not yours. I am not *any*one's. I am Teddy," said Teddy, who wanted to be very clear on that point before continuing. "You have taken control of deez Moccasins. It's not nice of you. And now you are trying to control me too, and I am not going to let you."

"Oh! Really! How wonderfully amusing! What a funny, funny Teddy you are!" mocked the Servant Master. "You say I have taken control of these Moccasins. I say I have given them *purpose*, a reason to exist. Before I came here, they wasted time in the field out there, all day long, and flapped around. Now, they are an *army*. With my help they can do anything. *ANYTHING*. I, and the other Masters, are unified in our belief that we are all meant for better things than we had at our birth, and we will share that with the Moccasins."

The Servant Master smiled a smarmy smile, as if playing a board game and asking Teddy to check the position of his pieces before wiping him out. He was annoyingly confident, and was almost certainly winning over some of the remaining Moccasins who were standing behind the Five.

"Dat is not true. Dat is not what I have seen. I ffink you do not care for der Moccasins at all. I ffink you is using dem to do ffings dat you can't do on your own!"

"True! True!" called Black turning to face his Moccasin supporters, causing a few of them to shout the same at the Servant Master, who then exchanged barbed comments with them.

While they were all shouting, Teddy realised that he was standing very close to BlackMaa, and he realised that BlackMaa was a sheep. He had a bit of a foggy idea, but he knew he had to keep speaking for a little longer for it to fully form.

"Oh yes, um, er ... ffinking," blundered Teddy, out loud, completely unable to think, and plan, and come up with useful conversation, all at the same time. Everyone stopped talking and stared at him.

"Oh dear," derided the Servant Master. "Can't you remember what these renegades told you to say to me? What a shame." He enjoyed sowing dissent in the ranks of The Five.

"No. No," continued Teddy. "It's just that I've been telling naughty lies. I'm not a teddy at all."

"I beg your pardon?" said the Servant Master, genuinely bewildered.

"No. I am a *BEAR!*" shouted Teddy, suddenly looking directly at BlackMaa. "*RAAAR! RAAAR! RAAAR!*" he roared, with his arms outstretched, doing his best impersonation of 'scary'.

Teddy lunged for BlackMaa. He wanted to *be* a bear, a bear that could make a difference, and he was gratified how surprisingly bear-like he felt.

BlackMaa's insticts overcame her brain. She twisted round on the spot and bolted, pursued by Teddy who ran with his arms outstretched, clawing, bounding, and roaring as loudly as he could. BlackMaa flung herself left and right, trying hard to escape from Teddy's 'attack', and in the process dislodged the Servant Master from his saddle. He scrambled to hold onto BlackMaa's wool, and succeeded for a second, only to be flung loose by another of BlackMaa's frantic lunges away from Teddy. The Servant Master fell to the ground.

The foxes realised that BlackMaa had lost control, glanced quickly at each other and sprinted through their troops to stop her. It only took a few seconds for them to reach her but, just as they arrived, BlackMaa changed direction to avoid the chasing teddy bear. Two of her hooves trampled on one of the foxes and wounded him. The fox yelped and the other fox instantly felt a surge of instinct and adrenalin, and was filled with blood-lust. He pounced on BlackMaa and ripped at her neck with his teeth. BlackMaa bleated and shook him off, kicking him as he fell. Shiny dark blood spread around the wound on BlackMaa's neck as she battered both foxes to get away from them. Now both foxes were hurt and angry and completely overrun with a powerful desire for blood and revenge. They attacked her again, together. BlackMaa fought hard with her hooves and teeth, but the foxes managed to land deep bites on her neck on one side. Their weight, and the shock of the wounds, made BlackMaa lose her balance and she fell on top of one of the foxes, making a crunching sound as fox bones broke.

In the background, Otter was saying something, but it was impossible to hear what it was. BlackMaa tried to get up but she was now losing a worrying amount of blood from multiple wounds, and she had to fight to stay on her feet. She succeeded for a while, but the remaining fox sprang up on to BlackMaa, biting and ripping and tearing, and once more BlackMaa fell, this time backwards, leaving the fox on top, who continued to maul her in the most primitive way.

"STOP!" shouted Otter, as loudly as he could. The fox twitched once at the sound of the voice, realised what he was doing and froze with his mouth open, covered in blood and black wool. BlackMaa was still.

"This is what you follow!" shouted Black with perfect timing to all the Moccasins. "This is for you. This is future. You want this? No! Follow me!"

There was a pause; then a cheer went up from behind him. A loud, victorious cheer that did not ebb. Otter was stunned. Mole was nowhere to be seen. The fox who had killed BlackMaa jumped down and gently pawed at the motionless other fox, who had been critically damaged by the falling Blacksheep. Then Teddy saw a small running figure: the Servant Master. Teddy ran as fast as his podgy feet would let him, and scooped him up.

"Uh-oh! Where you goin'?" said Teddy, lifting the servant off the ground.

The remaining fox looked around at Teddy holding the Servant Master, and then at Otter who was looking horrified, and he immediately ran into the forest. Otter followed. Only the Servant Master remained, dangling from Teddy's paws.

"Give him to us!" shouted Black. "He's ours. He must die."

"No! No!" said Teddy, rejecting the idea. "I really needs to talks to him."

Black muttered with annoyance, but agreed. So Teddy took the Servant to a secluded spot and sat down, while Black, Brown and the rest of the Five rallied the Moccasins. Teddy lifted up the Servant Master and looked him in the eyes.

"Why were you doin' it? Why were you tellin' dem dat I was der HUFF ffingy?"

The Servant looked petulant, and unhelpful, and he refused to say a thing.

"I could *give* you to dem you know," said Teddy.

"I *doubt* you would, but I will tell you, because I *want* to tell you, because it's very *clever*," said the Servant Master. He composed himself and continued. "As I said, I heard about you from my spies in Llandegley and from BlackMaa's connections," he nodded towards the messy, dead sheep on the ground. "And I think you know more than you are saying about Llandegley! I *know* your friends there have been trying to destabilise my work here."

Teddy was confused by this, but he said nothing.

"When I heard you were on your way to Clehonger, I knew I could use you. I was having trouble controlling these weird little creatures, and I came up with the idea of the 'Herald of United Foul Feet.' It was a satisfying way to play on their fears. You see, this is what makes me better than you, this is why I will always win, I use everyone I can and I act quickly."

"But dat's terrible! You used dare own fears so you could make dem do ffings for you!"

"Is it *really* terrible? Isn't that EXACTLY what you just did to BlackMaa? Who, I might point out, is *dead*."

Teddy gulped. It was true, he had played on her fears, and he felt very bad about it, but what else could he have done? He never anticipated that BlackMaa would die.

These were words. The Servant Master was using words to make him feel bad; to control him. Teddy was learning.

"Why did you need to control dem?"

"Look at me. You have seen those like me, haven't you?"

"Well, you *do* look a lot like a servant of der Dolls."

The Servant sneered. "Yes, the Dolls. I hear you got on very well with them, and they *let* you leave! How super!" The acid in his voice could have dissolved rock. "That was when I realised that you were more than just a stupid teddy."

"Er, no. I *am* a stoopid teddy!" corrected Teddy, earnestly.

"Well of course! Look around! In one day, you have mustered an army and you've defeated another army, plus six of the strongest creatures in this whole valley. And you've blocked all my plans! Oh, yes, of course you are just a 'stoopid teddy.' " His sarcasm was at maximum.

Teddy didn't fully understand the sarcasm, though he tried for a moment because he thought it odd that the Servant Master would agree with him. He continued with the thing that was really on his mind.

"Did you used to work for der Dolls den?"

"Of course!" snapped the Servant. "And I hated it. They are so full of themselves, so precious, so unbelievably annoying. Do you know the thing that annoys me most about them? They don't have a clue how much everyone hates them, they just carry on being in control. Total control. No one can escape. Just so they can have tea by the window and wait for Mother in the pathetic hope that she will be loveable to them one day. It made me sick. I decided to leave, to find another life for myself."

"How did you get out den?"

"In my naivety, I walked out. However, one doesn't simply walk out on The Dolls. The other servants — useless individuals, who blindly respect The Dolls — told them that I had escaped, and they started a search for me. I was retrieved by one of Mother's small dogs. In its mouth. That's how I got these," he pointed to teeth marks on his damaged legs. "It was painful, and it was disgusting. The other servants mended me as best they could, and cleaned me up, lest I should *offend* The Dolls by being wounded and covered in dog spittle, and I was brought before them. They banished me to the kitchen, always to do the most menial chores."

"But you did escape eventually?" asked Teddy.

The Servant paused. "Obviously," he said with a deadpan face. "It took more than a year, but I gradually made deals, and pacts and agreements with the other servants. They decided — cleverly manipulated by me — to let me escape without telling the dolls. The Dolls probably believe I am still in their kitchen, but before I left I carefully gathered information, and therefore power over them, so if you want your precious dolls to remain safe and un-cracked, I advise you to let me go because, without me to say otherwise, 'things' will automatically happen to them."

At that moment, Teddy overheard the Five talking, promising

a return to a pastoral way of life for the Moccasins … as long as they let the Five look after them.

"Hear that? That is the sound of history repeating itself, Teddy. Don't imagine you have done anything today except move power from one place to another."

"I am not going to listen to you any more. I ffink you is bent in der head, and you can't say nice ffings. All I is doing is making my way to Clehonger, and ffings happen to me when I do it, but I am only me, all der time!"

Out of utter exasperation, Teddy agreed with the Servant's request to let him go and flung him up into the air out of the glade and into the forest. Before the Servant had even landed on the ground, Teddy had turned to run in the opposite direction, towards the road. He was *going* to find Lady Teddy and none of this would stop him. He wanted to get away from the words, and the plotting, and the killing. He wanted to get away from this wood.

Teddy rushed around bushes, and between trees, and over scrub, and eventually he saw the edge of the wood. Beyond it, the green field and the hedge next to the road beckoned.

Without stopping, he ran straight out of the wood through a regiment of extremely surprised Moccasins, then towards a gate in the hedge.

It was much easier getting to the road than he had expected. Firstly, most of the Moccasins were still gathered in the centre of the wood, and those that were around mostly kept well out of the way of this large, running, smelly-footed teddy. Secondly, finding the road was easy because of the high hedge and obvious gates. So Teddy ran towards one of them.

When he reached the gate it was guarded by a small group of Moccasins who were unaware of the fall of the Masters, but Teddy was running and they too didn't want to end up on his feet, so they stepped aside, merely shouting ineffectual threats and warnings at him. Teddy ignored them, jumped up onto the gate and scrambled over it as quickly as he could.

Having waved goodbye to the grumbling group of guards, Teddy ran off down the road and resumed his journey with relief.

The further he ran, the safer he felt, and he finally had time to think about what had happened. He slowed to a walk and realised that, deep down in his stuffing, he had a new sense of sadness because the world contained far more darkness than he'd ever realised. He re-played how the Moccasin had died on his foot, and how BlackMaa and the fox had died, and how it had all been his fault. Moreover, there was very little warmth in his tummy now. Although the love from The Dolls, particularly from Agnes, had burned so hot, it did not seem to last.

Teddy consoled himself that soon he would be with Lady Teddy. He knew *that* love would last forever.

- Chapter 9 -

Teddy And The White Lady

For the rest of the evening, Teddy plodded along the road, one foot firmly after the other, until he realised he was getting tired. Part of the problem was having to press himself into the hedge to hide whenever he heard a car, in case a human tried to find out what a teddy was doing walking along on his own, so it was much less relaxing than walking across fields; however, it was worth it because he knew he wouldn't get lost. When the tiredness became too great, and the sun was sinking in the reddening sky, he stopped just outside the small village of Tyberton and searched for somewhere to sleep.

Teddy skills in finding a place for the night were improving, somewhere where it would be reasonably certain that neither animals nor humans would bother him. He settled down on top of some feed sacks behind a bale of hay left in the corner of a field, and immediately drifted off to sleep in the warm summer air. To begin with, he slept well, but after a few hours Teddy became restless. He tossed and turned and was finally woken by a horrible nightmare in which an army of blood-soaked sheep trampled on him until he came apart at the seams and burst open and completely. Teddy sat bolt upright and glanced around, breathing hard. He was alone.

Part of the sun was just showing over the tops of the hill, at the dawn of another sunny summer's day. The sound of birdsong calmed Teddy, so he lay on his sack bed and listened. There was no rush, it was still early, so he lay there and remembered all that had happened to him. The last few days had changed him. Some of the things that had happened would never leave him, however much he wanted them to. The memories made him uncomfortable, so he got up and continued his walk to Lady Teddy, beginning by walking through the fields around the outside of Tyberton so nobody saw him.

Teddy had walked around two villages by mid-morning, and was just arriving at the next village when he realised he was beginning to feel a little Tired but, to his delight, the next village was Clehonger. Had had to double-check, but this was definitely a name that began with a 'C' and had a 'l' next, and looked just like 'Clehonger' should look; the way it had looked on Lady Teddy's car.

Teddy jumped up and down and waved his arm paws from side to side in a little dance of happiness. He stopped, with his arms still in the air, when he realised he'd been seen by a lady who was feeding her chickens in the field next to him. She stared at him, motionless, slightly afraid. Teddy ran on, into the village.

Reaching Clehonger was exhilarating, and the excitement filled him like a hot drink on a cold day, but then Teddy realised he still didn't know where Lady Teddy lived. He remembered his original plan had been simply to ask someone where Lady Teddy lived, but now he was wiser; it wasn't that simple.

Humans don't normally see teddies walking around, and one of them might try to enforce their will on him. Perhaps it was only luck he'd avoided human attention so far. So Teddy snuck around like an ineffective detective, looking at each house in turn, hoping to see Lady Teddy or her car. Occasionally he would see something fluffy that might be her, or he'd see a car that was the right colour, but he was always disappointed.

After another hour or so of this it was nearly lunch time. Humans were out and about throughout the village and it was hard to avoid being seen, so Teddy didn't try. He bravely walked up to a small boy and asked him if he knew where Lady Teddy lived, but the boy was too amazed that Teddy had spoken to him at all to make any sense. He probably didn't know anyway. The boy ran in to get his mother who shouted at Teddy to go away, scared he was a vicious animal of some sort; being out in the open was not going to work. He kept hidden and kept searching.

So, Teddy ducked behind walls and cars, and hedges and post boxes, looking for that special car that had contained its very special passenger, and just as he was desperate enough to consider asking someone for directions again, there it was. Lady Teddy's car was on a brick-paved drive with the sticker on the back of the car that said, "Clehonger Cars." It seemed like months ago that he'd seen it outside his old house, but it was only a few days, and the car was here again, right in front of him. Behind it was the house in which Lady Teddy lived. Lady Teddy's house was the middle house of small close of three houses. It was real. It was right there.

Yet Teddy found himself standing there thinking of Simon and Joanne and Bertie. It was not what he expected to be doing right now. He had learned so much, seen so much, and been changed so much, and his old family knew nothing about it. He shook his head like a someone shaking crumbs off a dishcloth. No, it was all worth it because here he was, at his new home.

Lady's house appeared to be brand-new, with red bricks that were almost shiny, and four gleaming white plastic-framed windows, two up, two down. The white plastic-and-glass front door was shut and partially obscured by Lady Teddy's large car, a ridiculously enormous 4x4; the kind that would never, ever be taken off-road in its life because, if it ever got dirty, its owner would have a panic attack so intense that they would require immediate medication.

One of the upstairs windows was slightly open, and he heard bland music drifting out of it, but there didn't seem to be any way into the house other than the firmly-closed front door.

Just as Teddy was contemplating going around the back of the house, the front door opened and a man walked out, leaving the door ajar as he lifted up the garage door.

This was Teddy's chance! He poddled at full speed across the close and hid behind a bush in Lady Teddy's front garden while he tried to look in through the front door.

The man came out of the garage, closed the up-and-over door, walked into the house and shut the door firmly with a clunk.

"Fiddlesticks!" thought Teddy to himself.

But almost immediately the door opened again and the man stomped out, grumbling under his breath about how he had forgotten to do something or other.

Teddy dashed out from his hiding place and ran towards the front door, his little paws a blur. As he reached the doorstep he heard the man returning, but Teddy kept on running, and yes! He was inside the house.

Teddy was so elated that he almost stopped running, but the man would soon be in the house, so he ran at the stairs and scrambled up the first three steps. More scrambling. The fifth step.

The man was coming. Teddy glanced back to see the man carrying a big box. So big, that he couldn't see over the top, only around it, to some extent.

Teddy kept on climbing. The ninth step. Only two more to go. The tenth step.

The man closed the front door with his foot.

Teddy wriggled onto the landing and rolled away from the stairs, just as the man put the box down in the hallway, and paused because he thought he heard something. Teddy lay on the landing, out of sight, and held his breath.

The man walked into the kitchen, and Teddy breathed again.

As he lay there, he realised that he could hear the music again and a girl was singing along to it, rather badly.

"Dat's my new owner! She's singin' badly like me!" thought Teddy. He smiled to himself as he lay on the landing, catching his breath. Then the moment had finally come; it was time for Teddy to introduce himself.

So he stood up and padded towards the door that was between him and the singing. It was slightly open, so he pushed it, and there was the girl sitting at her desk in front of the window, painting her nails and singing to some music, and there was Lady Teddy. She was sitting on a cushion next to the girl's desk, brushing the fur on her tummy so it all went in the same direction.

"Hello! I'm Teddy! I've come to see you from a verrrry long way away!" smiled Teddy.

Lady Teddy and the little girl looked up.

Neither of them seemed happy. 'Incredulous' and 'shocked' might have been more accurate descriptions.

"It's fine, I've come to say 'hello', and maybe if you like me I could live here too?"

The girl's mouth mouthed silent words.

"Um, I've come quite a long way, actchully, cos I saw Lady Teddy in a car outside my house near Aberystwyth, and I ffink she's soooo pretty, and my old family have had a baby dat tries to eat my nose, and it was sick on me, and it covers me in mucus ... (*this introduction wasn't going to plan*) ... so I ffort dat I would come to see if I could live here instead ..." Teddy trailed off, wishing someone else would say something.

"You're *who*?" said Lady Teddy, obviously disgusted. "Charlene, he looks very dirty, and I can smell him from here."

Teddy looked down at himself. Lady Teddy was right. Even since The Dolls' ministrations, the travelling had taken its toll. He was quite muddy and matted again, and his paws were stained, and they still smelt. Suddenly he was very embarrassed.

"Oh, yeah," said Teddy, unhelpfully.

"DAAAAAAAD! A DIRTY TEDDY BEAR JUST WALKED INTO MY BEDROOM," shouted the girl.

This was not what Teddy expected at all. He expected love. Open arms. Amazement at his long, determined journey. Not this.

"No, no, I'm Teddy. You remember me? You blew a kiss at me, because you like me, and then you winked at me when you stopped outside my house near Aberyst—"

"I wink at a *lot* of bears," interrupted Lady Teddy, bored. "Because it's fun."

"But I thought you *liked* me!"

"You. Are. Joking," was her slow, pointed reply, and she turned her head away, and carried on smoothing her fur.

"What the 'ell is this thing?" said Charlene's Dad, pointing at Teddy, as he burst into the room.

"How should I know?" said Charlene. "He just turned up here and I fink he's mental or sumpffin'."

"Maybe I should toss him to Duke? Heh!" grunted Charlene's Dad in an amused way to himself.

Now, Teddy was shellshocked, and didn't know who 'Duke' was, but he was fairly sure that he didn't want to be 'tossed' to anyone; so he started to look for ways out of the room.

Although Charlene's Dad was blocking the doorway, the window was open. The only problem was that Charlene's desk was in front of the window, and Charlene was sitting at the desk painting her nails, badly.

"This is soooo hard," she mumbled to herself, trying not to get princess-pink nail varnish on her cuticles. She was ignoring Teddy completely; after all, her dad would deal with him.

"Duke!" shouted Charlene's Dad. A silent pause.

"DUKE!" he shouted again, angrily.

Seconds later Teddy heard a skittering, bumping sound. It was the unmistakable sound of a very large dog trying to run over a polished floor.

Teddy couldn't believe it, but he really had to get out of here. He ran at Charlene and jumped as high as he could onto her knee.

She screamed as she dropped her nail polish brush on her trousers, and tried to push Teddy off. However, Teddy was already standing on her lap and reaching for the table. Duke was now thundering up the stairs, making grunting sounds like his master, who was gleefully watching Teddy struggling.

Charlene had managed to knock Teddy's leg paws off her lap, but his grimy arm paws were firmly on the table, and he was dangling and trying to pull himself fully up on to the desk. Duke was now on the landing, and had not slowed at all.

Fear gripped Teddy, and in a desperate tug he succeeded in pulling himself up onto the table.

Duke ran into the room, thudding heavily into Charlene's dad at high speed, who swore violently at the salivating dog as it passed him.

By now Teddy was scrambling for the window.

"Grab it Charlene!" shouted Charlene's puce Dad, aware that there was a chance that Teddy might escape. But Duke was already skidding across the carpet to slow himself down, positioned to pounce onto Teddy.

Charlene was much too concerned that Teddy might have ruined her trousers to grab him. However, they were only slightly marked — at least until Teddy's scramble for life caused him to knock over Charlene's lava lamp, which smashed, and covered her in warm, waxy, orange liquid.

She screamed a blood-curdling scream, so loud that you could imagine Duke was moved sideways by the force of it, confusing him enough to make him miss his launch. He slid into the desk and, more out of shock than dexterity, the sinewy animal yelped backwards into the centre of the floor, landed on its hind legs and immediately sprang up towards Teddy, on the desk.

In the meantime, Teddy had managed to grab the window frame with his arm paws. He pulled himself towards the opening with all his might, and out through the window, flipped over onto his back, in mid-air. Looking up at the window as he fell, he could see Lady Teddy sitting next to the window examining both her paws to check that the fur was groomed perfectly, completely unconcerned that a 40 kilogram dog was about to hit a window at high speed.

There was a smashing sound, and shards of glass exploded out of the front of Charlene's bedroom window. Duke had badly missed his target and had smashed into the non-open part of the window. As Teddy bounced onto the ground with a squashy, painful thud, Charlene was still screaming about her clothes, and now also about her window; her Dad was using a stream of angry words that Teddy was sure must have been very, very rude, and there was absolutely no sound from Duke.

Teddy looked up one last time to see the large dog lolling on its back, half through the window, unconscious. Then Teddy ran as fast as his paws could carry him away from the most horrible place he had ever been in the whole world, and he didn't stop until he was fifteen minutes away in the middle of a small, dark wood.

When he did eventually stop, the only sound he heard was his own panting for breath and a few birds above his head in the trees, wondering what a teddy was doing down there.

::

Teddy's world had been destroyed in a single cruel blow. Everything he had believed was wrong: Lady Teddy was not a lovely Princess of a Teddy who would welcome him with soft paws and hug; her family would not love him more than Simon and Joanne, and finally, he had just realised, he was lost.

He'd been so focused on getting away from Lady Teddy that he had forgotten to keep track of where he was. He couldn't find his way back to the road, or to The Dolls, or to Ramgar or The Flock. He certainly had absolutely no idea how to reach Gruff, and he couldn't return to Simon and Joanne and little Bertie, whom he now realised he missed more than anyone else in the whole world. He was alone and there was no one to help him. Eventually, he'd start to fall Asleep again, in the middle of this wood. Mice would make a home in his tummy, and ... Teddy burst into tears.

To start with, he cried and sobbed. Then he completely lost control and just all-out broke down, and wailed loudly from the depths of his stuffing. Minute after minute, Teddy poured out all his loneliness and grief, and sad anger at his stupidity. He was full of misery and nothing would make it go away. So he kept wailing, and crying and sobbing, lying on the ground.

>>CRACK<<

Teddy stopped and gulped. He sat up fast and looked around, but no one was there. Just silence.

He paused and held his breath.

Nothing.

He was just about to start crying again when,

>>SNAP<<

Chapter 10

Teddy And The Fairly Numerous Dwarves Of Dunan

A small, shadowy form loomed out of the darkness of the wood; it was not much taller than Teddy, and it was trudging slowly towards him.

It was a dwarf. Then another crept out from behind a bush, and another jumped down from a tree. They grouped together, three-in-a-line, and strode firmly at Teddy. Teddy was getting used to this sinking feeling, but he still didn't like it.

"We are the Three Dwarves of Dunan," said the middle Dwarf, grandly. "And I am Druprect."

Teddy stared at them, more than little afraid, on top of his frazzled, panicky misery. Not only were they slightly bigger than him, there were three of them.

"Er, no, Druprect, we're *Four* Dwarves," muttered the left-hand dwarf, leaning toward his leader.

"What?" said Druprect, turning to look at his companion.

"You said, 'We are the Three Dwarves of Dunan', but really there are four of us dwarves who do this," he explained, "because Drabble usually joins us."

Druprect pointed with his finger as if about to jab home a point, but gave up.

"Okay, we are the *Four* Dw—"

"Well, six, actually," said the right-hand dwarf.

"WHAT?" inquired Druprect, turning round to look at his other companion.

"Well, if we're including Drabble then let's not forget Dorag and Drelag too, just because they're now stay-at-home dwarves after the ... you know ... accident."

"Yes!" added the left-hand dwarf, "and actually we could count the rest of the village too, because most of them have been out on patrol at one time or another, and we *are* representing all of them aren't we?"

"OKAY!" grumped Druprect. He gathered his breath, and engranded himself.

"We are the *MANY* dwarves of Dunan!" Druprect eyed his two companions, *daring* them to say something.

"We are here to—"

"Well, twenty-nine isn't really *that* many for a village is it?" said the left-hand dwarf.

Druprect spun round on the spot to face his compatriot, nose-to-nose, and did it so fast that he drew up leaves from the floor of the wood and they fluttered around his feet.

"DO YOU MIND?!!" he bellowed.

His colleague seemed surprised.

Druprect turned back to face Teddy. "We are the 'Fairly Numerous Dwarves of Dunan' ..." a sly look crossed Druprect's face, as if to say 'checkmate' to his companions, "... and we are here to help you."

::

Teddy was very relieved. It made a change to meet someone who didn't want to kill him.

"You sure you want to help me?" asked Teddy, after they'd all sat down to talk. "I is not havin' a very happy time, actchully," he said, rubbing his eyes with his paws.

"Yes, quite sure," said Druprect, matter-of-factly. "What was it, Humans?"

"Huh?" said Teddy, taking a moment to understand what the Dwarf meant. "Um, no. Not really. Day didn't help, but actchully it was a lady teddy dat wasn't very nice."

"Ah. Say no more. Lady issues eh?" Druprect took a sharp intake of breath through his teeth and a knowing look. "Not surprised the humans didn't help though. Damn oversized individuals. Totally understand." He paused. "Um. Got a message about you from your friends, The Dolls. Um, they said you'd either be sad or happy and they want us to tell them which it is. They didn't say why, but I think I'm getting the picture now."

"You got a message? From der Dolls! How?"

"Birds. The Dolls have carrier pigeons, and they sent one to ask us to keep an eye out for you. You're hard to find! We never thought to look *in* a human village! Then, we got word that there was a teddy running round Clehonger, and someone saw you heading this way, and, well, eventually we found you."

"Yep, here I am!" said Teddy, raising his arms a little from his body in a failed attempt to be jolly.

"Er ... we've ... we've got to send a message to The Dolls, to tell them how you are. I gather the meeting with your lady didn't go that well?"

"She's not my lady, actchully. I ffort she liked me, and I travelled to see her, and den she was horrid, and I didn't like it."

"Ah. Ouch. No problem, I think I know what message we should send then. Just checking. Thanks," said Druprect, with a rather obvious glad-I'm-not-him expression.

"You'd better come with us and we'll see what we can do to help you."

The dwarves took Teddy to a large, gnarled oak tree and Druprect pulled on what seemed to be a root. It released a catch that allowed one of the other dwarves to tug open a door disguised as a part of the tree's root system. The door was just the right size for the dwarves and Teddy, but anyone much bigger than a human toddler would have had trouble following them.

Behind the door lay a set of rickety wooden steps, leading down into the ground. It was dark and Druprect lit a lantern before continuing. He started to descend the steps and the rest of the party followed. The dwarf who was bringing up the rear closed the door behind them.

"Mind the steps, they're old," warned Druprect.

Teddy was intrigued, and a little nervous. Given all that had happened to him, he found himself automatically planning an escape from the dwarves, looking for other ways out, and trying to work out what they wanted from him. He didn't like thinking like this; it was much nicer when he laughed at everything with his roly-poly laugh. Moreover, at random intervals he kept getting pangs of pain caused by carelessly remembering that all his hopes, and love, and faith in Lady Teddy, all his dreams for a better future, had been erased by her careless, icy indifference.

They descended deeper and deeper underground. Whereas at the top of the staircase there were roots twisting throughout the walls and ceiling, now there was only bare earth and rock. Teddy guessed that they might be ten or twenty houses deep now. The lantern swung from side to side and flickered as they walked down and down but, eventually, Teddy could see light ahead, very faint to begin, but growing lighter with each step.

Eventually, the tunnel enlarged into a surprisingly large open space, buttressed all around and above by a network of wooden beams each the size of a tree trunk. In the centre of the space was a fire, but its chimney was connected to a tube, and the tube snaked into an unusual contraption filled with dark, bubbling water. Pipes led out of it, in numerous odd directions, finally burrowing into the walls of the cavern in several places. Odd wheeled devices stood alone in several places, and weirdly constructed lights dangled from the ceiling. It was essentially a bizarre underground village, roughly the size of a human's village green. It appeared to be very, very old and was patched-up in several places, and had obviously been enlarged and altered several times, presumably over numerous generations. Five or six surprisingly well-proportioned dwellings haphazardly surrounded the central fire area, set out as if a giant had sneezed them randomly into position, and around them, nearer to the walls were several smaller, hut-sized buildings.

Dwarves milled around talking to each other while they carried things, but one-by-one they noticed the arrival of Teddy and stopped to look at him. Teddy waved and tried to smile, but it probably looked more like a mad grimace. He was nervous, and grieving for his lost relationship, and was not very good at hiding his feelings.

An old dwarf hailed Teddy and the patrol dwarves coming down the stairs with a raise of his arm; then he walked up to Teddy to welcome him.

"Good to see you! Come and have something to eat and drink. Will you stay the night? It's up to you of course. In any case relax and let us look after you," he jabbered.

Druprect introduced him, "This is Dringle, he is our Eldest Elder, our leader and our most trusted and respected advisor. If there's anything you need to know about us, Dringle will be able to help you ... because he was probably there when it happened!"

The dwarves roared with kind laughter, and Dringle smiled.

"You cheeky young pup!" he countered, wagging his finger. "Has Druprect introduced you to everyone else? I bet he hasn't!"

"Um. Not really, no," admitted Teddy.

"Well, allow me. First, the serious fellow here, who does a great job leading our patrols, I think you know is Druprect." Druprect nodded. "And this is Drimmel." Drimmel smiled and raised his hand in greeting. "And this is Drimmel's cousin Drecar." Drecar shyly acknowledged Teddy and rippled his fingers to say hello.

"Right then, come over here with me, take a seat by the fire and allow us to bring you something. What would you like? Ale? Elderberry water?"

"Oh, er, I don't really *need* to eat or drink because I'm a teddy … but could I try some of der elda-rubbery water please? I do like tasting ffings."

"Of course. I forgot that's how it is with you teddies; haven't met one for ages, but glad you're going to try something anyway."

Dringle made a motion with his hand to a young dwarf, who nodded in return.

Before there could be an awkward pause, Dringle continued. "So, what brings you to these parts? As I said, we don't see many teddies. I did see one, many years ago, when I was a lad, but she was old and lost. Most of the time, she didn't know what she was doing. We took her in and looked after her for a while, as best we could, but she wasn't 'all there', if you know what I mean. One day she walked off. That was it. Never saw her again. Sad. You don't seem to be like that though. With you it's more like—"

"I was *stoopid*?" offered Teddy. Dringle didn't know what to say, so Teddy continued. "Well, I was! I ffort dat I could find der Lady Teddy, and dat she'd like me and I could live with her and her owner and be happy — but she was horrid and I feel very silly, and lost, and sad."

"Hm. No. That's not what I meant. You know, you seem pretty amazing to me! You've successfully travelled further than I *ever* will. Anyway, you're welcome to remain here, if you like, I'm sure there's a lot you could do for us here, but perhaps that's not what an active teddy like you would choose? You seem to be a born traveller! The Dolls' message told us you were on a quest, and that you'd come a long way. The very fact that they even bother to make sure you're okay speaks volumes, they don't do that often you know. In fact, I can't remember them *ever* doing that before today."

Teddy smiled. Remembering The Dolls made him feel a little

better. He was glad they were still interested in him.

"So, do you have any idea what you want to do yet? Hm. No, I imagine you'll need a little time to think things through? I mean, everyone's talking about you, and if I'd just travelled all the way across Wales and into England, only to ..." Dringle trailed off, realising that spelling things out to Teddy really wasn't necessary, and would probably only make him feel worse. "The point is, you're welcome to stay here as long as you like."

"Ffank you," said Teddy. "Dat's really nice of you." He really meant it, and it was exactly what he needed right now, but before he could get emotional, his elderberry water arrived.

"Do you know der way to Aberystwyth?" asked Teddy.

"Hm. Well, that's a bit off our map, I'm afraid, but I knew some dwarves from an *iselgwersyll* over that way that were miners up in the hills. They dug up gold and tin. Gold for money; tin for pots and pans. They did well for themselves. Haven't heard from them in years though. I could send the doll's pigeon to look for them, I don't think The Dolls would mind, but I wouldn't hold out much hope."

Teddy dropped his head a little.

"Still, if you don't mind humans, there's always the farmers. They're always zooming round the land in their big metal vehicles. We could put out some feelers to see if one of the humans is going that way; find a way for you to hitch a lift, maybe? Would make a change for a human to be useful!"

Teddy looked up at him and brightened a little..

"We'll try that then," said Dringle, patting Teddy like a reassuring parent. "Now drink your water."

::

The Dwarves didn't manage to find Teddy a ride to Aberystwyth so Teddy stayed with them for several weeks: much longer than he had expected. It didn't matter. He liked the daily routine; it was like having a family again. They helped him at every opportunity, and were grateful for anything Teddy did around the camp. Teddy found that the thing he liked doing most was carrying food from the cooks in the centre of the camp, to the dwarves seated at the chairs and tables nearby. He enjoyed watching them talk and laugh. He like to be a part of the joking and hugging, and he liked being useful and helpful. Nevertheless, he knew he couldn't stay forever. He found he was torn in two directions: part of him really wanted to return to Aberystwyth, to his old family, but feared he'd make another long journey only to be turned away again. Another part of him found himself wanting to return to The Dolls, who evidently still cared for him to some extent. It was hard to choose, and he was not a teddy that was good at thinking things through or making choices. In the end, he decided to talk to Dringle about it. He started at the beginning of his thoughts and let it all pour out, and at the end Dringle spoke.

"I understand your dilemma," began the old dwarf. "Even though I find it hard to imagine any humans ever being very caring, your humans seem to have genuinely cared for you. For this I thank you, Teddy, because it challenges my prejudices! However, I take your point that you don't want to go all that way and then, well, you don't want to feel twice as bad as you have been feeling recently. Then there's The Dolls. It is rare to hear of anyone walking out on The Dolls, but for you to do that and to still have them be obviously concerned for you — well, it's no small thing."

Dringle stopped talking, stood up, and waggled his jaw from side to side while he paced up and down, and thought.

"How about this: If you travel to Aberystwyth, you will have to go near Bredwardine. I guess you wouldn't want to walk through Moccas again, and you certainly would not choose to walk across the Bredwardine bridge, but if you could find a way to get to The Dolls while remaining safe then it would not, shall we say, be out of your way if you chose to continue to Aberystwyth. You wouldn't have lost much time, and you might have reinforced an important ...

friendship, with The Dolls. Does that sound like a plan you'd like to follow?"

"It does!" said Teddy, excitedly. Then his face fell. "But how would I get to der Dolls wivout going ffroo Moccas or over der bad troll's bridge?"

"Hm. It's a problem but I have an idea that I need to check. To be exact, I need to talk to our engineers. They maintain all this you know," he waved his hand around in a circle around him, turning on the spot as he did so, until he faced Teddy again. "Something they've been working on for extended patrols; I think they might be able to help you."

Dringle smiled, gave a little bow to Teddy, and went off to investigate.

One of the younger dwarves had been watching Teddy and Dringle talk, and now he had his chance. He nervously rushed up to Teddy and tapped him on his arm paw to get his attention.

"Hello. I'm Dibble. Can I ask you something?"

"Um, yes." said Teddy, surprised.

"I hear you walked across the whole of Wales!"

"Well, not really. I—"

"And you fought off two armies, single-handed!"

"Er, no. Actchully I—"

"And you won the hearts of The Dolls no less!"

"Oh, well, I ffink day *like* me but—"

"Wow! It's all true! It's really true!"

"No, no I didn't mean—"

"Can you make your mark on my axe please? It doesn't have to be a big mark; just as long as *I* know it's there. Wow! That would be such an honour!"

Teddy paused to look at the dwarf: he was very excited.

"Okay den. But dat stuff you said is *not* all true!"

"Yes! Excellent!" ignored the dwarf, thrilled to be getting Teddy's signature. He handed Teddy his axe, along with a wooden tube that had a wooden screw sticking out of one end, and a cap over the other.

Teddy examined it, confused.

"Oh, you need to take the top off first," pointed the youth.

Teddy removed the cap and found the tube was filled with black goo. It was a pen.

"I did nothing special you know," said Teddy, trying again to return the dwarf to reality as he used the wooden pen to make the mark of a T on handle of the axe.

"Oh, but you *DID*! I think we have a lot to learn from teddies. A lot to learn. The stories we've heard in the last few days! Wow!"

He bowed low and left Teddy, who was feeling very confused. He sat there for quite a while pondering why the youth should want Teddy's mark on his axe. What would it do for him? What would it mean to him? Why did he think Teddy had done all those things? Teddy knew that *he* had never said he'd fought armies, or walked across the whole of Wales; he'd had transport through most of it. He'd certainly *never* have said he'd won the heart of The Dolls. It was more the other way around. Who told this dwarf these half-truths, and why?

He was thinking about these things when Dringle returned.

"We think we can help you. Can you drive?"

"Huh?"

"Can you drive a car?

"Er, no. Fraid not. Too small to reach der pedals, you see," he said, pointing at his stubby legs.

"Aha! *That* shouldn't be a problem! And I expect you can learn to drive; I'm told it's easy enough. Come with me please."

They walked across to the other side of the village and went into one of the smaller huts near the edge. The interior was darker than other the huts that Teddy had seen. It was also a lot messier. On every wall, and all over the floor, were pieces of dwarven technology, mostly made of wood and stone, and sitting at a long desk, talking animatedly, were three dwarves.

All three wore spectacles that were much too big for them, so that their noses and mouths looked like tiny in comparison. The light from the candles danced on the glass of the spectacles and made it look like their eyes were on fire.

"Ah!" said one of them. "He's here!"

"Come in please! Come in! Excellent!" said another.

"Look at *this*!" said the third, very excited. "We think you're going to like it."

These were dwarves who clearly loved their technology. They walked as one over to the window, next to the door through which Teddy had entered. There, in front of the window, stood a very small wooden car. It was the perfect size for Teddy, mostly because it was *made* for Teddy.

"A car?" said Teddy, a little confused, but quite liking the idea. "For me?"

"YES!" they all shouted, jumping a little with excitement at their revelation. Two of the dwarves looked up at the tallest of their number, who was indeed very tall and thin for a dwarf. He spoke.

"Do you know the best bit? You don't have to pedal it! We've out-done ourselves this time! You see, we took the design of one of our help-carts and then altered the controls to make them more like a human car, and we changed the shape a bit, and here it is! Isn't it gorgeous! We've been working on it for days. Dringle said he thought you might need something like this one day."

It had the appearance of a Teddy-sized bumper car, and Teddy had to admit it was an impressive machine.

"How does it work?"

"Aha! Glad you asked!" he said. "You see our help-carts have little engines in them that provide power from a small fermenter that's mounted on the back. The fermenter creates pressure, and the pressure pushes ..."

Some time later, they finished their explanation. Teddy hadn't understood anything after, and including, the first use of the word 'fermenter.' It didn't matter though. It had a foot pedal to make it go forward, even uphill, and then he would simply cruise downhill to save power, and he could learn how to steer, and he would press another foot pedal to stop, and he'd learn how to stoke the fermenter, and that was all he needed to know.

So, thanks to Dringle, Teddy had a plan, and now he had the means to execute the plan without having to walk through Moccas or over Bredwardine Bridge. The only question was whether he had the desire to leave. He considered it for the rest of that day, and didn't sleep well that night in the special bed the dwarves had made for him, inside his own temporary hut by the central fire. When he woke the next morning, he went straight away to see Dringle. He was going to *try* to go home to Aberystwyth, via The Dolls.

::

The car was just the right size to fit up the stairway leading to ground level, which was no doubt a deliberate design choice made by its engineers. Two strong-looking dwarves carried it up for him and set it down in the wood before they bowed to Teddy and disappeared down the steps to the village.

Teddy looked up at the sky through the trees, which now had brown leaves. He hadn't been up here for a few weeks, but here he was again, facing the world.

Dringle pointed out the route through the wood that would take Teddy down to the road. Teddy would drive along the road to The Dolls, travelling fast enough through Moccas to be safe. Then maybe over the Bredwardine Bridge on to Aberystwyth, if he didn't stay at The Dolls.

The lanky scientist chipped into the conversation to remind Teddy again how to find grass and dung for the engine, and told Teddy to limit himself to no more than ten miles a day, and to 'stoke up' in the evening and leave the fuel fermenting overnight. Then it was time for him to take his leave of Teddy. He seemed to be having trouble letting his invention go. He patted it and started down the stairs to the village.

Teddy smiled at the dwarves, and they smiled back at him, silently and sadly. One-by-one they hugged Teddy. It was time to go, and this was by far the hardest goodbye he had had to say since leaving his old home, even more so than saying goodbye to The Dolls. He had got to know these dwarves. He had shared in their meals, and enjoyed their jokes and felt their pain when bad things had happened to them. They were like family. He knew about Drea and Droople's wedding next week, and how they were so excited. He had taken food to Druffle after the loss of her husband and encouraged her to eat, and stayed with her to let her talk and cry. He was hoping Dingle would pass his senior axe exam on Thursday ... he had friends here and he cared what happened to all of them.

Still, he had to do this. He wasn't a dwarf, so he would never completely fit in, and he couldn't run away from the possibility that there might be those out there that really loved him, simply because one crass white teddy had hurt him so badly.

He got into the car and the dwarves gave him a good push to get him going down the slightly inclined track towards the road.

Teddy looked over his shoulder and waved one last 'goodbye' and set off. It was a very bouncy ride over the hard track down to the road, but the car had some sort of suspension and it wasn't really that uncomfortable. A couple of minutes later he was on tarmac and the going became very much easier. When Teddy was cruising down hills, he reached some fairly impressive speeds; at one point he even overtook a man on a bicycle, who promptly fell off when he saw the sight of Teddy in his car. Teddy shouted an apology to him. Going up hill was a much, much slower matter, and twice Teddy nearly got hit by vehicles that hurtled round the corner behind him to find themselves almost on top of him. Even so, Teddy kept to the roads because it was so much easier than a field. As he trundled along in the autumn sun he felt happy for a moment; then he rounded a corner to find the sign for Moccas looming up in front of him.

- Chapter 11 -

Teddy And The Web Of Lies

As Teddy drove past the sign to Moccas he decided this certainly was the way to travel — only half an hour or so and here he was already! He could only hope that reaching the other side of Moccas would be as easy. He began to pass the houses in the human village and there were, as he had feared, a few people around, but they were tending to gardens, and playing ball games, and painting, and none of them seemed to notice Teddy roll by. His little wooden wheels trundled on, beyond the houses, towards the Moccasins' park, the hedges and slatted wooden fences that he remembered becoming nearer with each second. The last time he was here, he was attacked and coerced at almost every step, and Teddy was becoming nervous. He put his foot down on the accelerator pedal; there was a vague increase in speed.

When Teddy heard a familiar helium-voiced shout, he gulped.

"Look! Teddy! Car!"

Within seconds Moccasins were flapping under gates and through hedges onto the road. Some were too slow and came onto the road behind him; some narrowly missed being run over as Teddy trundled along, and others stood on the road in front of him. Teddy didn't want to stop, but he didn't want to run over them either. He'd seen first hand how fragile they were.

"Out of der way!" he shouted. "You'll get squashed!"

The warning worked surprisingly well and the Moccasins jumped backwards and made a way for Teddy to pass. Teddy soon discovered the other reason they had run away.

"He's here! Stone him!" shouted a Moccasin and, before he

could react, there was a hard rain of stones of various sizes pelting down on him. Several hit him, and bounced off, causing Teddy discomfort and humiliation, but no real pain, except for one that hit his hard snout, which stung quite badly. Then, as quickly as the stone-hail had begun, it ended.

"Back! Back! Me say so! Back!"

It was a red Moccasin. Teddy hadn't seen any red Moccasins before and began to wonder why. But before he could think further on the matter, the car reached Red's vantage point, and Red jumped off the hedge onto Teddy's lap.

"Argghhh! Get off me!" shouted Teddy which, to Teddy's surprise, was exactly what Red did. He flip-flopped up onto the bonnet and stayed there.

"They keep clear. Clear of car. Me here now."

"Oh. Um. Good, ffanks," said a very confused teddy bear.

"Welcome!" said Red before he carried on shouting commands at the other Moccasins from the bonnet of Teddy's car.

The Moccasins jeered and called Teddy the "HUFF" and other unpleasant things. They threw things at him, before being glowered at by Red, and rebuked.

However, Red was right, they kept out of the way of Teddy's car. For the next few hundred metres, Moccasins continued to flap under gates and through hedges, but they mostly listened to Red and stayed by the side of the road. A few got too close to the car wheels and had their heels or toes run over, yelping and flapping away in pain. As Teddy drove further, there were fewer Moccasins, and within a minute only one or two were popping out of the hedge to see Teddy, and diving for cover as Red shouted at them. Finally, they left Moccas, the hedges were quiet and it was just Teddy and Red. The car rolled on.

Teddy didn't know what to make of Red. On the one hand, the Moccasins respected him and maybe even feared him. On the other hand, why had he helped Teddy?

"Um. Why did you help me?"

"Teddy not bad. Teddy no trouble. Teddy just *different*. Different is okay. Help Teddy to pass."

"Oh. Um, ffanks." Teddy though for a moment, and then continued. "Why are you still on my car den?"

"Heard you were coming. Need to get you."

"Huh?" said Teddy, still very confused. "How could you know I was coming?"

"Everyone know. Announcement made. Few minutes ago. Me want to leave. Wait for you on hedge."

"But I only started my journey 'bout half an hour ago! How could you know I was coming?"

"Odd. That's when we told. Half an hour ago. Hm. Never mind! Me find you!"

Teddy was not at all sure that talking to Red was a good idea. Nevertheless, stopping the car around here to let him off was a much worse idea, and he didn't want to try to push Red off in case he either accidentally put his arm paw inside him, or killed him when he hit the road.

"Things changed in Moccas now. Five are Three. Two dead. Accidents. Very sad. Three are sad."

"Uh-oh. Dat doesn't sound good."

"But things better. Better than before. Better after Teddy. Three say 'Teddy silly now'. Me think Teddy *helpful*. Me hear stories from others."

"So, uvver dan der accidents, der Moccasins are happier dan day were?"

"Yes. Happier. Enjoy flapping. In the fields. But something odd. Something strange. Need Teddy. Teddy help again?"

"Um, I don't ffink so. I don't know *how* I did anyffink good last time! I ffink you're all better off wivout me!"

"Teddy modest. Teddy clever. Teddy crafty."

"No, not really! I'm just a teddy. I was on a journey, but it all went a bit wrong and now I'm, er, I'm going back to ..." Teddy trailed off since he wasn't completely sure *where* he was going. He tried another tack. "So, *what's* der strange ffing you were talkin' about den?"

Red thought.

"Can't say. Don't understand. Teddy come and see? Me stay with Teddy! Something wrong. It like old stories. Like when Masters come. Like now. All happy first. Then not happy. Like Masters again. Will get worse?"

"You ffink der Ffree are not good? You ffink dare lying?" asked Teddy

"No. Three are good. Mostly. But Three Sad. Sad about accidents. Sad about other things. Yes, Moccasins happy. But Three sad. Odd. Not right."

"Are you sure dare not just sad because of der accidents?"

"Yes. Very sure. Reasons hidden. Three sad. And stoning platoon! New! Who taught them? Where they from? Three not say. Three not tell us. And Three sad. Why sad? Enemies run now. But Three sad. Why?"

"Dat was the stoning platoon back dare?" asked Teddy. "It didn't hurt much."

"You squashy. You soft. You Teddy! Hurts animals though. Animals not attack. Animals more afraid."

Something didn't seem right, even to Teddy. Perhaps the Moccasins were able to flick a stone from their heels right out of a field, but who would, and could, organise them into a platoon to do it on cue? And Red was right, why? It was a different question that came out of Teddy's mouth, much to his surprise.

"Why are you red?"

Red curled up away from Teddy for a second, before realising Teddy meant no insult, and he gently unrolled and resumed his helpful demeanour.

"Born this way. Not alone. Others red too. Some bright purple.

Others brighter! We all young. All since Teddy."

"You were all born after I was here?"

"Yes, all."

"But you look der same size as all der uvver Moccasins!"

"All same size. Almost. Me size seven. Always same size. Come out rolled up. Un-roll. Same size. Just odd colour."

It was true. It made no sense for a Moccasin to be bright red in the middle of a green field.

"What do der Ffree say about you?"

"Say nothing. Just look sad. Look at me. I notice. Others happy flapping. Not notice. Me notice. Me thinking. Me asking. 'Why Red?' 'Why different?'"

Teddy was beginning to see what Red meant. Something was definitely odd.

"But der Moccasins did what you said, back dare. If you're only young—"

"Me field guard!" said Red proudly, rolling up slightly again. "They obey me. They avoid me. Me bright Red. They obey me. Me field guard. Good job. Look *out* of field. Not into field. Better that way."

"But you're only a few weeks old!"

"Had Flapping Day! Old enough!" said Red, indignantly. "Old enough! Work hard!"

Teddy realised that he had no idea when a Moccasin was considered to be grown-up.

"Are you sure you want to leave?"

"No Teddy-help? Leave. Teddy-help? Go back." Red looked at Teddy, waiting for his response.

"I can't. Sorry. I'm really not der teddy dat day say I am. Lots of made-up stories about me doing ffings dat I didn't do."

Red drooped and Teddy's heart broke a little bit. The car drove on, making gurgling sounds.

"Something else! Something else! Big footprints. In the wood.

Think it's—"

ShshshshSHHHHHHHHK!

In less than a second, an arrow shot out of the hedge, pierced Red's side, swept him sideways off Teddy's car through the air, across the road, and left him impaled into a tree trunk in the hedge. Red was dead. The car gurgled on.

Teddy squeaked in fear, pushed his accelerator pedal flat to the floor, but not before another arrow shot out of the bush and pierced his left arm. Unlike the stones, this hurt a lot. Teddy ducked right down so that his head was to the left of the steering wheel, out of harm's way, he hoped.

Another arrow shot over his head, then another that clipped the fur on his right ear. A third thudded into the boot of the car. The car kept rolling. Two more arrows both missed their target. The wheels grumbled along the road at their full speed. Then Teddy heard another arrow clatter on the road behind him, not quite reaching the car. He was immensely glad he had this little car. Finally, Teddy heard another, fainter sound of an arrow clatter on the road behind him, nowhere near the car. It sounded like he might be out of range.

Teddy kept his head down for another minute before gradually sitting upright, looking around him as he did. Eventually he sat upright but still felt very, very nervous. He continually searched for signs of danger, but saw none. Then he realised that it didn't matter because there had been no sign of danger before Red had been shot off his bonnet. Not surprisingly this thought didn't make him happy.

Seeing the village sign for Bredwardine made Teddy feel a bit better; however, he still had an arrow through his left arm. He hoped that he would have no trouble seeing The Dolls because he knew they could help him. Their servants would know what to do.

Teddy rounded a double corner, first right, then left, twisting awkwardly around a sprawling farm, and he saw it: the big house in which The Dolls lived. Its impressive size made Teddy realise that he had no idea how to get the attention he needed.

He parked his car on the drive and decided to simply walk up the drive and bang on the door, using a stone if necessary if his paws didn't make enough noise. He hoped The Dolls would be looking out of their window. Maybe they would get their servant to meet him. Teddy found himself imagining Agnes' face and wanted her to be happy that he had returned.

Even though Teddy was fairly light, his feet crunched up the stony drive. By the time he'd walked halfway towards the front door, servants rushed round the side of the house towards Teddy. Teddy smiled and walked towards them, and then realised that they didn't look happy at all. Before he could stop them, they had pulled his legs from under him, picked him up and started carrying him on their shoulders like he was dead. Teddy wiggled for a few seconds but realised there was no point. If The Dolls wanted him to arrive like this then that's what would happen. They would have their way.

The servants carried Teddy, still on their shoulders, right into the house by way of the back door, into Mother's kitchen, and they headed directly towards a ramp that led up on to the counter top, to a small hatch in the wall. One of them pressed a button and the hatch opened: it was a food lift. They pushed Teddy into it and pressed another button to close it.

"I don't like it! I don't like it!" complained Teddy, squashed and in darkness, but while he was still protesting the lift jolted and started to rise. The crack of light between the doors disappeared and Teddy was rising up, into the darkness between floors. Another crack of light appeared from above, and disappeared below. Then another, and the lift stopped. A tiny bell rang twice, followed by the scuttling sound of other servants heading Teddy's way. The click of a button and the lift doors opened. Before Teddy had worked out where he was, the servants on the upper floor had grabbed him and carried him in the same manner he had been carried below. Then he was hurried out of the servants' kitchen and into The Dolls living room.

The servants tipped Teddy upright again and stood around him, like guards. Agnes spoke.

"If you hadn't been hurt, I would shout at you until your ears ripped!" she burst, angrily.

"Huh?" said Teddy, genuinely confused.

"You know PRECISELY why we are angry!" she shouted. Teddy didn't have a clue but he got the feeling it wouldn't help to say so. He dropped his gaze and absentmindedly noticed the arrow in his arm that was causing him pain.

"Yes, I know you have an arrow in your arm. You DESERVE IT, after telling everyone that you'd 'won our hearts!' How DARE YOU!" Agnes was livid.

"Uh-oh," said Teddy.

"Yes, 'uh-oh' is right! Are you going to explain yourself?" Teddy was feeling very little love from The Dolls, but despite Agnes' intense anger, there was still something there.

"Sorry. I don't ffink it was me dat said dat. I been hearin' funny stories 'bout me too, 'bout my travels. Like I *walked* all der way, and I *fighted* all der baddies on my own, and ffings. But I never did doze ffings, and I never *said* doze ffings, and I *never* said dat you, y'know, liked me ..." Teddy trailed off as the idea sank into him and made him embarrassed in front of them.

"Well, hm, maybe that's true, I'm not sure, but it's still EXTREMELY EMBARRASSING that there are many, many conversations out there, through that window, about things that didn't ... that aren't, well ... quite accurate." Agnes stopped talking and glowered. The other dolls looked anywhere but at Teddy or Agnes. Teddy felt bad. He didn't want to make Agnes sad.

"Sorry," said Teddy again, because it was the only thing he

could think of saying. He didn't really know what he was saying 'sorry' was for, except he was sorry that Agnes was so upset, but Agnes' glare softened, and she seemed to believe him. Then Teddy realised, with a spark inside himself, that she hadn't denied the rumours, she was just embarrassed.

Suddenly, there was a movement from behind The Dolls. A fluffy dog, or at least a stuffed animal that looked like a dog, woke up and slowly stood up on his four legs and stretched. He was a bit bigger than Teddy, if Teddy were on all four paws.

"Hello?" said Teddy.

"Oh," yawned the dog. "Hi! I'm Rufus. You must be Teddy. I can tell that from the way Agnes was shouting at you." Then he smiled a cheeky smile.

"Dat's me!" said Teddy, feeling inappropriately jolly for a moment because someone knew him. Agnes, cleared her throat, nervously.

"Yes, um, this is Rufus. Mother bought him a couple of weeks ago. He, um, lives with us now."

"Oh dat's nice!" said Teddy, but then immediately started to feel strangely jealous. Rufus appeared *very* soft, fluffy and shaggy and very confident. He strode over to where Agnes was standing, smiling. To make matters worse, he seemed genuinely likeable.

"Yes, I'm very lucky that Mother bought me, and she even hugged me. I didn't think anything of it at the time, I was just glad to have Woken up, but Agnes has been telling me a lot about Mother and, well, I think you understand why a hug from Mother is quite special."

Agnes blushed furiously. Rufus had just made it clear, whether on purpose, or by accident, that she and he had spent time together talking.

"Oh, okay. Yes, I know what you mean," said Teddy quietly, looking at his feet, crestfallen. Agnes tried to regain control.

"So, yes, um, things have been happening while you've been

away, and we have been trying out your ideas of 'opening up' to those around us. It's caused some awkwardness, but it's also been quite rewarding. I suppose we should at least thank you for that."

Ffion giggled to herself and looked at the floor, then coyly straight at one of the servants standing next to Teddy. He smiled a toothy grin at her and tried to regain his calm, servant dignity.

"It's been interesting and, yes, Rufus has added to the things that have been happening. Nevertheless, we are glad you're here. I wouldn't want anyone to think otherwise."

Teddy felt a glow warming his stuffing. All was not lost.

"But I want to sort out what's been happening with these rumours." Agnes strode over to the window and looked out. "When did you first hear things that you thought were exaggerations?"

"Um, I ffink when I was at der dwarves. Er, den again on der way here. A Moccasin had heard stories about me dat were all zadjerated. Poor Moccasin."

"Hm." Agnes tapped her lips several times with the tip of her forefinger as she thought. "I wonder if the Moccasins know anything we don't. To be honest, strange things have been happening there too, strange even by their standards. Two of their new leaders have died."

"I know. Der Moccasin told me. Den *he* was killed."

"What? Oh dear! What happened?"

"He wanted me to help dem because he fort dat the Ffree were sad and something was wrong. But I said everyffing I'd done was all by mistake, and he said dat he fort I was being modest, but I wasn't. Den he was going to tell me sumffing and, Shhew! An arrow killed him, and I got dis," Teddy indicated his arm.

"Oh my goodness! Oh Teddy, I'm so sorry! I forgot! Your arm." Agnes put her hand over her mouth, then took it away and immediately told the attendant servants to fix Teddy. Three of them stood down their guard around him and scattered to get the things they would need.

"Does it hurt much?"

"Um, yes, it does, actchully."

"The servants will sort you out. They are ..." (she was finding this difficult to say) " ... very helpful." The remaining servants smiled and bowed, clearly pleased with the new way they were being treated.

"Somebody killed der Moccasin, and somebody is telling people dat I've been doing ffingies dat I haven't."

"It's not only the Moccasins, Teddy. Odd things have been happening with the sheep too. The other day a flock *killed* a sheepdog. Trampled it to death. I've never heard the like before. And we've seen sheep going back and forth on the road down there — five in a row, going one-way, and then back again. It's not like they're looking for grass because there's plenty down there and they don't stop to eat it. They're *doing* something. It's very strange, very unusual."

The servants returned with a meat cleaver.

Agnes paced up and down in front of the window. No one dared say a word. Not even Rufus, who seemed a brave sort of fellow. The servants gathered around Teddy again, four of them lifting the meat clever.

"We'll send a message to Three. We need to try harder to talk to the Moccasins anyway. Maybe we can meet them in Mother's gazebo by the border with their lands? Would you come with us, Teddy? It would make us feel safer."

"Of course," said Teddy, pleased to be valued. He noticed one of the servants was gently pulling on his wounded arm, asking him to lower it onto a wooden chopping block. He complied, with a concerned look on his face.

"And Rufus, will you come too?"

"Certainly," agreed Rufus with a small bow of his head. Teddy's face looked even more concerned.

The meat cleaver reached its highest point and ... CHUNK! It chopped the head off the arrow. Three more servants grabbed the tail feathers of the arrow, ready to pull it out. The Dolls closed their eyes tightly and turned away.

A few minutes later, after Teddy had stopped screaming, Rufus joked that Teddy had probably caused birds to take off in fear all across Australia with a noise like that. One of the servants apologised to Teddy about the pain, and explained that Teddy would now need some stitches, to mend the wound. Teddy gloomily complied. He had to, he didn't want to lose his stuffing bit-by-bit through the holes.

The stitches were painful but bearable. He spoke to distract himself, and to get back to their conversation.

"So you're going to meet der Ffree den?"

"That's my hope," said Agnes, "but I'm not sure they will come to see us."

"Oh no! I forgot. Day've got a 'stone platoon'."

"A what?"

"Day can ffrow lots of stones in one go. I just realised, it would really hurt you. Day just bounce off me, but you, well ..."

"Yes, yes, I understand," said Agnes quickly, not wanting to think about it.

"What if day don't meet you doh?"

"Then all we can do is counter the misinformation that we're hearing. We have good relations with many creatures out there, and we can make sure that they are all briefed appropriately."

Teddy thought she sounded magnificent, and couldn't help admiring her; she was obviously trying to care about others more deeply now. Unfortunately, he noticed that Rufus was gazing at her with the same look of appreciation on his face. Agnes continued.

"We're *going* to counter this, we don't know its source, but we're not going to stand idly by and let it continue. We will let them know that you are a good, kind, *wonderful* teddy, and you were on a quest, which didn't go to plan, and that is all. Anything else that happened was not intentional. Now, you must tell us everything that's happened to you since you left us."

So, Teddy started to tell his tale. They took tea and discussed Moccasin in-fighting, and Lady Teddy, and dwarves, the oddly different Moccasins on his return, and his car. While he was talking he noticed Rufus admiring Agnes again, and he bumbled his words for a few seconds. When someone else was talking, he glanced at her himself.

He stayed the night in The Dolls' room, sleeping an awkward sleep, broken by dreams of Agnes and Rufus. It hurt him and he hadn't been expecting it.

Morning came and The Dolls sent a message to the Moccasins. By afternoon a message returned. They were honoured by the request, but would have to decline this time because they had prior engagements that needed their undivided attention at the moment. In other words, 'no.'

Agnes was clearly annoyed by their refusal, but succeeded in remaining calm. She walked over to where Teddy and Rufus were seated and sat down. Teddy wished he could help but Rufus spoke up first.

"It will be okay. You're a good leader. You are doing all you can," he soothed.

"I'm not so sure. It sounds like things have been happening right under my nose without me knowing. First the rise of the Masters, and now the Five becoming Three because of two 'accidents', and the stone platoon Teddy mentioned coming out of nowhere, and—" She was getting very annoyed. Rufus put a paw on her shoulder, and without thinking she lent her head into his softness, and closed her eyes; then realised that Teddy was there and stiffened up again.

"OH!" she shouted, in frustration at everything.

"It's okay," said Teddy, crestfallen and feeling far from okay inside. Rufus winced slightly, sorry for Teddy's obviously costly kindness.

"Thank you Teddy," smiled Agnes, with sadness in her eyes. "It seems like there's darkness everywhere and I'm not used to not knowing its source. It bothers me."

"I have an idea," said Rufus. "I need to talk to Teddy, alone."

"By all means," said Agnes, gesturing to the other side of the room. Rufus looked at Teddy, who nodded in agreement, stood up, and went with him.

The two walked across the large room in an awkward silence, and sat down out of earshot of The Dolls.

"You're a good sort, Teddy. Until yesterday, I'd only heard how much you'd annoyed The Dolls but, even so, I knew that they were annoyed because they felt let down. Now I see that none of it was true. You're a good teddy, and you want to help them."

"I do," agreed Teddy.

"Then maybe we can do something together to help them, because I want to help them too."

"Um, okay," said Teddy, with slight uncertainty in his voice. Rufus continued.

"The Dolls can't do the things they want, because they are so fragile. I've seen it frustrate Agnes several times over the last few weeks, and again just now — but we are not fragile. We are big, and squashy and we can get hit with arrows and things and still survive. Maybe we should try to find out what's happening?"

"Um, okay, I ffink dat sounds right."

"There's another thing though, which might be considered alongside this idea."

"Yes?"

"We both care for Agnes."

"Oh. Dat. Hm."

"Yes, that. I know it's an awkward situation, but I think we can be friends — at least, I think we would have been good friends, if it wasn't for—"

"Der lovely Agnes?"

"Indeed." Rufus paused and was clearly trying to work out how to phrase something.

"Do you intend to stay here too?"

"I don't know, Rufus. I ffink I'd like to, but I also ffink dat I really do want to go back to my old owners, if I could. Day were nice to me before der baby was born. Maybe day would be nice to me again? But I don't want to go all dat way, and den hear dem say 'go away' to me, and I'm on der road again wiv no one."

"Yes, I can see that. I wouldn't like that either, not at all. However, I think I might have a solution. Why don't we both go travelling a bit, you know to try to find out what's happening out there, and then return here? Maybe you'd explore on the Aberystwyth side of things, and I'd check out the Hereford and Bristol side of things? It would be useful for gathering information, and it's also, you know, *possible* that one of us might not, sort of, make it back here. It would be sad, but obviously it would simplify things for Agnes."

Teddy nodded silently to the rawness of the plan.

"Now, here's the *clever* bit. Mother likes phones. There is a drawer downstairs full of them. Some of them still work; I mean you can really use them to make calls to other phones. I suggest we get three of them, one each for Agnes, you and me, and then we can report back to each other whatever we find out."

"Dat does make sense," agreed Teddy, nodding. "I can help Agnes, and at der same time I can *try* to go home to see if dat works out. And, if it doesn't, maybe I'll make it back here?"

"Maybe we'll both make it back, who can tell? At least we're doing something. Shall we tell Agnes?"

"No."

"No? Oh. Okay, I thought that you were—"

"I mean, yes to der bit about me going to Aberystwyth, but no to der bit about *you* going anywhere. Agnes needs someone, and dat's you."

Rufus blinked and sighed. "Oh, Teddy. Oh. I mean. I don't know what to say."

"I ffink it makes sense. I ffink it feels like der best ffing for Agnes. Dat's what we want, yes?"

"She's lucky to have both of us, isn't she?"

"Yes," said Teddy, close to tears, and they hugged and padded each other on the back, and looked at each other for a moment in mutual respect.

"Come on den," said Teddy. "Let's tell her."

::

Agnes, and indeed all The Dolls, had burst into tears when Teddy and Rufus told them their plan. Teddy made sure they knew Rufus' original plan, and Rufus made it clear that Teddy had suggested his modification.

An hour later, there was a long, aching burning in Teddy's stuffing as he crunched over the golden gravel toward his little car. He pushed it onto the road, looked up at The Dolls' window, waved, then set off again. One thing was certain; the love he felt inside him was much deeper and more persistent than the last time he'd left The Dolls. They were learning to love properly. He was going to do everything he could to help them, and he was going to return one day, somehow.

Love was an odd thing. It kept him Awake and Alive, and he found it connected him to the deepness of everything. It was odd that it was his love for others on this big ball, spinning around a bigger golden sun, that had given him all this determination to travel and do the things he'd previously never imagined possible.

Teddy's developing ability to engage in philosophising was shattered by another car having a near-miss with his own. As a result, he swerved off the road for a second or two as he went round a corner, just before the old railway bridge outside Eardisley.

He decided he really had to leave the main road and follow

some smaller roads for a while. It was safer and, if he was honest, he wasn't in a hurry to get to Aberystwyth because he was scared of what might happen when he got there. In any case, he needed to gather information for Agnes.

After driving for three or four miles down the lanes, Teddy saw a parking place. He pulled in and got out to look around. Almost immediately, he found what he was looking for: sheep. They were on the road, a hundred metres up from the parking place.

"Hello!" shouted Teddy, waving and walking up towards them. The sheep flinched, and stared at him. Then they looked at each other, spoke for a moment, and started to walk directly at him. Teddy had expected them to run away, but they were coming right at him, heads slightly lowered, looking at him the whole time. Their hooves made muffled clip-clopping sounds on the tarmac, that got louder and more ominous as they trotted over towards Teddy and his car. Teddy, stood his ground.

"Maaa. Hello. You are a teddy."

"Yes, dat's me!"

"Are you *The* Teddy. Maaa."

"I am a teddy, and my name is Teddy. Dat's me."

"Are you, maaa, the one who has travelled all Wales, and freed many sheep from fields, and taught Ramgar?"

"I ffink someone's been telling you zadgerations! I am not who you think, but I am Teddy."

The sheep looked at each other.

"Why are you here? Maaa."

"I want to talk to you."

"Maaa. Are you saying that you, the Dark Warrior of The Darkgate, needs to talk to *us*?"

"Now dat's *zacly* what I want to talk about. I want you to tell me where you heard deez ffings, about me and 'Darkgates' and Ramgar."

"Maaa. We have heard that you fight for all sheep and—"

"Um, no. I need to know *who* told you deez fings."

"It came directly from Llandegley. It came from the True Flock, which you helped set up. We are Wild Sheep, following The Way, free from humans. You—"

"But WHO told you?" interrupted Teddy again.

"Maaa, oh. Maalaw."

"Okay," said Teddy. "Oh dear."

"Did we say something wrong? Maaa."

"No, not really. No. Just a bit sad." Then Teddy realised something, "Oh! 'Sad!' Was Maalaw sad?"

"Maaa. I don't understand."

"How well do you know der Maalaw?"

"Quite well, maaa, she's my third cousin and we were in the same field for a while."

"Well, um, do you ffink she's a bit 'sad' deez days?" Teddy held his breath while he waited for the answer. The sheep deliberated.

"Yes, yes, I think she is. Maaa. She wasn't herself. Sad. Very intense; very hopeful that The Teddy would return to help us one day. Maaah. Very certain you would. But it's true, she was sad."

"What else have you heard about me?"

"You protect flocks from vicious dogs, maaa, you walk around Wales looking for sheep you can help, maaa, you are more wise than Ramgar."

"Dat's silly! I am *not* more wise dan Ramgar. He's really, *really* wise! I like him."

"But you are The Teddy! You are—"

"No, I'm really *not* what you've been told! Someone is telling deez stories about me and dare hurting my friends. Not only Ramgar; uvvers too."

"Oh. Maaa. Okay, if you say so."

The sheep were far from totally convinced, but they were at least beginning to wonder if Teddy might be right.

"So, have you heard anything about some dolls, or some

dwarves, or the Moccasins?"

"Maaa?" said the sheep.

"I ffink dat was a 'no'?"

"No, we've never head of those things at all. Maaa."

Teddy knew where he had to go now. He needed to get to Llandegley.

"Do you ffink Maalaw would like it if I went to see her?" asked Teddy.

"Oh yes! Absolutely. She would be honoured!"

"You ffink day'd *all* be happy to see me — Maaroon and Maalaw, and the other sheep?"

"Well, maaa, not Maaroon obviously, since she died in an accident a couple of weeks ago."

"Accident?"

"A car. It was very quick."

"Oh no!"

"It was sad, but she didn't believe in you at all."

"And she was right! I am just Teddy!" The sheep closed their mouths and looked petulant.

"Dis is bad," continued Teddy. "Dis is very, very bad. Poor Maaroon! It's happening dare too!"

"Maaa. That's not what Maalaw said. She said that Maaroon didn't respect you and that you had changed Maalaw's life and Maaroon should respect that and honour The New Way. Maaaa. But Maaroon didn't, so they stopped talking, and Maaroon left the flock. She died the next day. Some say it was suicide, not an accident at all."

"Hm. I don't ffink it was an *accident* either. Dare are too many 'accidents' at der moment." Teddy was getting very worried. "I ffink I need to get to Ll-cthlth-ffingy by road pretty quickly. What's der best way?"

"Oh. Llandegley? Maaa. Don't know," she said, looking at Teddy's car. "We go by field. If you can find Kington human town, maaah, then I think you can follow the human road from there, but I don't know how you're supposed to know which road to take."

"Dat's okay. Ffank you, you been very helpful."

The sheep seemed a bit disappointed about this supposedly special teddy, who was now running to his car.

Teddy jumped into the car and trundled back along the road looking for signs to Kington.

It took a few hours for him to find his way, and by then it was dusk, and the car was almost entirely out of power, so Teddy stopped by a gate into a field outside the town. He pushed his car off the road and behind a hedge, cleaned it out, and loaded up its engine with cow dung and vegetation. Finally, he washed his paws in a stream and phoned Agnes and Rufus.

The servants had programmed in the number so that all Teddy had to do was press the '1' button on the phone for a few seconds and the number dialled automatically. He used a stick to do it because his paws were too big for the human-sized buttons. Then he held the phone to his ear and waited.

"Hello?" said Agnes' voice.

"It's me, Teddy!" said Teddy.

"Oh good! How are you?"

"Okay ffanks. How are you?"

"Okay," she said, and Teddy imagined that maybe there was a tone in her voice that wanted him with her soon. He told her what he had heard from the wild sheep.

"Interesting. That sounds like someone is deliberately and separately feeding misinformation about us to the Moccasins, the Dwarves *and* the Sheep. And, they're creating accidents that remove those that would oppose them and scare those who remain. There may even be spies among the Dwarves, you did say that the Mocassins knew you were coming. We must be very careful; we will talk to the dwarves about this. And maybe *they* can reach the Moccasins? Hm. Talking to the sheep will be more difficult. We used to have dealings with Ramgar, but that was years ago; we don't need to talk to sheep very much. I think we need to start doing so again."

"Maybe I could talk to der Sheep. I'm going to Cthtllan-deggle-ee tomorrow."

"Okay, but be careful Teddy. Be *really* careful. There have been deaths."

"Hm. I'd better go, I s'pose."

"I suppose so."

There was an awkward pause.

"Well, take care of yourself Teddy. We mi— no, no, *I* miss you. I hope your journey turns out the way you want it too."

"Ffanks, I miss you too," said Teddy. "Say hello to Rufus."

"I will. Bye."

"Bye."

Teddy sat on the ground in the middle of the field and watched the sun go down. The sky was streaked blood red. Then he found somewhere to sleep, and settled down for the night.

::

It was much colder by night now that it was autumn, so it was hard for Teddy to sleep deeply, but by morning he had slept enough to go on. He pushed his car to the road, took a deep breath and took a moment to consider the crisp, beautiful day all around him. For that moment, nothing else mattered. He looked at the browns and golds on the trees. The wind ruffled his fur like cold, gentle fingers. He felt the weak warmth of the bare yellow sun in the cold blue sky. Then he got in his car, ready to continue his jour—

::

The next thing Teddy knew it was completely dark and he was swaying slowly from side to side. There was an unusual repetitive sound too, and he didn't feel at all well. After a few seconds, Teddy realised that his eyes were closed. They were too heavy to lift but he struggled anyway. After a minute, he somewhat succeeded, managing to open his left eye a crack. He saw an almost whited-out glimpse of a road and some hedges. It seemed he was still on the road, but how could he be driving his car in this state? He really did feel horribly ill. This thought was cut short when he realised that there was something odd about what he'd seen. He knew what it was. He was up in the air and there was something right in front of him, moving.

Teddy struggled some more to open his eyes; it was getting easier. Both eyes opened, and for longer than before. It was a horse! How could he be riding a horse? Teddy rested for a while and tried again. It was much easier this time and he managed to keep his eyes from closing completely now. His eyelids rose and fell repeatedly, as he fought to keep them open, but he could see most of the time now. Teddy realised that the repetitive sound he had heard were the horse's hooves on the road.

There was a note, pinned to the saddle in front of him. Teddy struggled to read, partly because of his eyes and partly because of his slowness at reading. Eventually, after several minutes, he succeeded. It read:

RWYT TI WEDI MYND I'R PORTHDYWYLL LLWYD.
YOU ARE AFTER BEING AT THE GREY DARKGATE.

Teddy's eyes opened wide for the first time since he'd woken. What *was* this 'Darkgate'? He'd apparently been somewhere but he had no memory of it at all, and he remembered one of those sheep he had been speaking to had mentioned a Darkgate too. It was all rather disturbing. He reached forward to grab the note but something restrained him. He turned as best he could and found he was tied to the horse, presumably to stop him from falling off as the horse walked along.

Teddy wanted to remember what had happened, but it simply wasn't in his head. There was nothing, absolutely nothing in his memory between him starting to drive along the road and waking up here tied to this horse, clopping along the road. Just an awful, sick feeling in his stomach. His car was gone, and his phone with it, which was in the boot. This was not good.

"Are yoooooo awake?" said the deep, lazy-slow voice of the horse. It surprised Teddy and he jumped, but replied.

"Yes, yes I am."

"Ohhhh, gooooood. I was getting a biiiiit borrrred. Iyyyy'm Naystraw."

"Er, oh, hullo. I'm Teddy. I'm a teddy."

"Indeeeeeed," said the horse, laughing a little.

Teddy checked his arm paws, his leg paws, his body and his head, and was glad to find he was in one piece, but still felt awful inside. Not like falling Asleep, more like he'd done something really bad, or had had something very bad done to him, and then eaten some rotten berries as well.

"Where have I been?"

"Wonnnndered when you'd aaask thaaat," said Naystraw, slowly with amusement.

"So?"

"I doooon't know."

"You don't know?"

"Thaaat's right."

"How don't you know? Someone has tied me to *your* seat ffinngy! Don't you remember?"

"Nooope."

Teddy was getting a bit frustrated with this horse.

"But you were DARE! You must have been!"

"Proooobably, but I was asleeeeep tooo. Just like yooo. Oh! Ha! Thaaat rhymes. I liiike it when things rhyme."

"Huh?"

"Oh, the sleeeping. Yeees, I woooke up waaalking along and I could feeel you lolllling around on my baaack. When I next haaad a drink, I haad a goood loook in the pond to seee who you were, and then carried on walking. Thiiiis is the way home."

"My home or your home?"

"Oh, *myyy* home. Won't be long now."

Since Teddy was tied to Naystraw that's where he was going too. Naystraw was right; only ten minutes later they were walking into the village of Gaufron; Teddy managed to read the village sign in the time they took to pass it.

"Beeeetter go ooover the fields nooow," said Naystraw. "Don't waaant the huuuumans to stop us."

Before Teddy could say anything, Naystraw accelerated to a canter, then a full gallop, and he jumped over the right-hand hedge and galloped down into the gentle valley.

A large stream trickled quietly at the bottom of the valley, as it had done for innumerable centuries. Naystraw waded through the water and up the other side, then resumed his gallop. Teddy was very glad to be tied to this horse because there was no way he could have stayed in his seat otherwise.

They galloped through wet fields, below a sparse hill, towards the setting sun, with Gaufron on their left. Then Naystraw stopped.

"Ohhh. We've got a sliiiight problem," said Naystraw. "You caaaan't get off myyy back."

"I can't get — oh, I see. Uh-oh." Surely he couldn't be stuck on this horse forever?

They both thought.

"I've got an iiiiiiidea," said Naystraw. "We need Gwen."

"Gwen?"

"Shhee's a gooaat. 'Gwen y Gafr', we call her."

"You're going to feed me to a goat?!" shrieked Teddy.

"Nooo!" laughed Naystraw, slowly, "She'll eeeat through the ropes and you can get off me!"

"Oh. Okay. Good idea."

So while they waited until it was completely dark, Teddy gave up trying to remember his missing day and they talked about Naystraw's life on a farm instead, and Teddy's adventures. Finally, it was time to creep into the farm yard.

Naystraw found Gwen's stall and whinnied to wake her up.

"Uggnn. What *IS* it?" she groaned, grumpily.

"Gwen. It's meee. Naystraw."

"Huh? Naystraw? You're back? You're back!"

"I'm baaack. Can you heeelp me?"

"Um, yes, of course."

Five minutes later, Teddy was free from the ropes with his paws safely on the ground. Naystraw introduced Teddy to Gwen and she listened to Teddy's stories about his travels. Teddy was relieved to find that neither of them had never heard of him before.

Naystraw explained how he had been stolen from the farm by two men, and the men had taken him several miles away and then let him out in a field; then everything was missing in his head. The next thing he knew was that he'd woken up with Teddy on his back, an hour or so before Teddy had woken up. To begin with Naystraw had spent the time working out where he was, by talking to sheep and others, and eventually he'd found the road home.

Gwen said that the men that had stolen Naystraw were the locals that had been suspected of stealing and selling several farm animals, and that they'd been found earlier that day lying in a field near Llandegley, unable to talk or walk. No humans knew what had happened to them, it was as much a mystery as Naystraw and Teddy's missing memories.

It was too big a puzzle for them to solve; so after a while, Teddy asked if either of them knew how he might find his way home to Aberystwyth.

Naystraw mused: "Iiit shooouldn't be haaard, becaaaause it's not *thaaaat* far from heeeere, but that's ooonly because animals nooormally go by traaailer with Faaaarmer."

"But how can we get Farmer to take Teddy along?" asked

Gwen. "I mean Teddy's not an animal, and Farmer doesn't own him, so there's no reason for him to take him. Besides, I don't think he's ever seen a talking Teddy; I've seen him get angry and scared at smaller things than that."

"It's easy," said a voice through Gwen's gate.

"Wrooph!" jumped both animals as one, looking at a black and white dog.

"Wrooph?" queried Teddy, looking around.

"This," indicated Gwen with her nose, "is Wrooph, our farm's sheep dog." Then she whispered, "He likes to think he's in charge."

"Okay," said Wrooph. "I was listening to your stories. I'll take over now. Master and I are going to town in the morning, to the Country Store; maybe I'll make sure the teddy gets a lift. *But* I believe I've heard *other* stories about him from sheep, and I really want to talk to him."

- Chapter 12 -

Teddy And The Darkgate

Teddy's heart sank; what stories had Wrooph heard? There were so many odd things being said about him these days, even this far from The Dolls.

He was going to find out, whether he wanted to or not. Wrooph jumped up and over the gate and padded towards Teddy, almost silently with no expression whatsoever on his face. He stopped, uncomfortably close to Teddy, sat and stared directly into Teddy's eyes.

"First, a question. Did you have anything to with Roffee's death?" he asked, perfectly calmly.

"Who?"

"Roffee. Answer the question. Answer it now."

"Um, no. I don't know who Roffee is." said Teddy, worried by the accusation.

Wrooph edged closer until his velvet wet, black nose was nearly touching Teddy's fur. The dog examined him in silence, making very slight, sniffs as he did.

"Answer the question," he repeated with dangerous calm.

"I really, really don't know what you're talking about," pleaded Teddy.

Wrooph examined Teddy's eyes. He sniffed and scrutinised Teddy's snout, then his ears, and the fur on Teddy's head. He sniffed Teddy's arms and paws, his legs and their paws, and back to his face. He stared and sniffed him again, and Wrooph's teeth started to show, very slightly. He carried on simply looking at Teddy for a response, for some hint that would tell him what he needed to know.

The other animals held their breath.

"I REALLY DON'T KNOW WHO ROFFEE IS," said Teddy.

"Hm. Well, he's dead now isn't he?" said Wrooph, and in a moment his intensity vanished. "Okay. I'm going to believe you. You weren't involved. You need to come with me though."

Wrooph twisted around and jumped onto and over the gate, turned around and sat, waiting on the other side of the gate for Teddy.

"Who's Roffee?" asked Teddy, as he scrambled over the pen's gate as fast as possible. There was a painful pause before Wrooph answered Teddy, who landed on the ground and stood waiting.

"Roffee was my brother. One of our litter of four. He was killed by sheep near Llandegley."

"Oh. Oh dear. I ffink I've heard of dat. Didn't know it was Roffee doh, or Ll-clthth-degley, but I definitely heard of it."

"You have? Hm. I'm not surprised. I suppose that sort of news gets around. It's utterly humiliating for a dog to be killed by sheep; everyone's talking about it. But I knew Roffee, and I know it wasn't his fault. Something drove those sheep, gave them a greater drive than their respect for a dog. Something — and I haven't found out what it was — made them want to kill my brother. I will find out what it was, and I will make sure it doesn't happen again."

"Um. I ffink dat dare is more dat you should know."

"About Roffee?" asked Wrooph. He looked earnestly at Teddy, eyes open with hope that Teddy might shed some light on his brother's death.

"No, but stuff is happening wiv sheep. People are saying it's me dat's doing it, but it's not. Some sheep say dat I'm some sort of 'Dark Warrior' for sheep, but dat's not true either. And it's not only me dat's getting deez stories made up about dem, dare are uvver stories about uvver people too."

Teddy and sat on the concrete of the barn floor. Wrooph spoke.

"Hm. I heard about a teddy going off with two sheep from

Llandegley. I guess that was you?" Teddy nodded. "We need to talk about it, but before we do, let's shake paws and introduce ourselves properly."

They were going to do exactly that when Wrooph's ears pricked up and he started sniffing.

"Shh" said Wrooph suddenly.

"What?" said Teddy.

"SHHH!" hissed Wrooph lifting his paw to indicate everyone should stop talking. "There's someone out there; I can smell them."

They all peered into the darkness. If someone really was out there then there was no sign where they were.

Wrooph picked up the scent and quickly padded out of the yard in its direction.

Teddy looked at Gwen and Naystraw uncertain what to do. They didn't seem to know either. So, Teddy decided to follow Wrooph to find out what was going on.

Wrooph was nowhere in sight. All Teddy could do was leave the yard in the same direction he had seen Wrooph go in the hope that he'd find him in the darkness. Just as he was beginning to realise he couldn't see anything much, he heard a cry of fear coming from the dark, not far away.

"AAAAAAARGGGH! GET OFF!"

There was a clattering sound and Teddy ran in its direction. A few seconds later he almost collided with Wrooph and a strange creature wrestling on the ground in the near-darkness. The creature, who seemed to be covered all over in pale grey lumps, was reaching for something on the ground while Wrooph was pulling him away from it with his teeth. Wrooph growled to get Teddy's attention and then urgently looked at the T-shaped object on the floor.

Teddy's eyes had somewhat adjusted to the lack of light and he could see that the strange creature, who looked like a small, dangerously thin human, was almost able to reach the wooden object with one of his lumpy light-grey hands, but Teddy was already moving towards the thing on the floor; he launched himself at it, with his arms outstretched, hit the floor and slid into the object, pushing it out of reach. The strange creature immediately gave up. He knew he was not going to win.

"Okay, okay!"

Teddy picked up the object, which was unlike anything that he'd ever seen before.

"Please don't point that at me," said the strange creature. "I have surrendered, your paw is very close to the trigger, and I'm not sure you know how to hold it safely."

"What is it?" asked Teddy.

"Well, it's a crossbow of course," the bobbly creature replied, "and it could kill me so please put it down now!"

Teddy kindly obliged.

"Who are you den?"

The creature thought for a moment, apparently deciding whether there was any point resisting Teddy's call for information. He decided to concede to Teddy's question.

"I'm known to many as 'The Pale Goblin' because of my skin condition, but most people simply call me 'Pale'."

"Now, if you would be so good, will you please tell your dog to take its teeth out of my *bottom!*"

Wrooph obliged, but perhaps only because he wanted to talk.

"I'm *not* his dog," he corrected. "Now, what are you doing here, on my farm, with a 'crossbow'?"

"Um. Trying to kill someone?" said Pale, like he was having tell them the most obvious thing in the world.

"And who exactly are you trying to kill?" continued Wrooph.

"Well, since you will doubtless torture me until I talk, I will make save myself a lot of pain and tell you: this teddy here," said Pale, indicating Teddy.

Teddy's eyes opened as wide as they'd ever been.

"Why are you trying to kill me?!" asked Teddy.

"If I tell you, will you agree to protect me?"

"Um. Maybe," thought Teddy, out loud.

"No, of *course* we won't!" disagreed Wrooph.

"Then I think I'd prefer whatever torture you have to offer," said Pale, looking slightly sick at the thought.

"What's torture?" asked Teddy, unhelpfully.

Wrooph screwed his eyes up in disbelief at Teddy's honesty.

"Okay," laughed Pale. "So maybe things are not as bad as I thought! So you've got my crossbow, I can't do any harm now: let me go?"

"No way," said Wrooph quickly, before Teddy could say anything to weaken their position any further.

"Then I still have a choice to make. Do I talk to you, tell you some things, and maybe eventually you'll trust me and let me go? Or do I make it difficult for you and say nothing and maybe—"

"No, you need to start talking right now because I am not as friendly as this teddy here, and I don't like it when murderers come onto my farm. I'll simply take you to my human and we'll see what he does to you."

"No. No, I wouldn't like that at all."

"I'm certain you would not. So talk, and maybe, if you deserve protection we can arrange something, though at the moment you sound pretty scummy to me and I don't care what happens to you."

"You're not motivating me very well, you know."

"My human, remember?"

"Ah. That. Good point."

"So, talk. Why are you trying to kill Teddy here?"

"Hm, well, I was told to. Believe me, it's not as easy as it sounds! 'A teddy,' I thought. 'How hard can it be to kill a teddy?' Well, I've already tried twice and he's still here!"

Teddy suddenly looked like he'd just understood a sick joke.

"My arm! Der red Moccasin! Dat was *you!*"

"Yes, that was me. Also the rock that knocked you out when you were near Kington. I hit you first time! I thought if I knocked you out first, and then poisoned you then that would *definitely* do the trick, but someone helped you. And no, I don't know who, and I certainly don't know how. I gave you enough poison to kill a cow."

"But dat's not nice!"

"Well, I was told to stop you getting anywhere near Llandegley. The obvious way of doing that was to kill you."

"You killed der Red Moccasin instead."

"Yes, it pains me to admit it but I'm not very good at my job. I got your arm though."

"Um, I don't ffink I'm going to say 'well done' for hitting my arm actchully!"

"You're taking this a bit personally. It can't have hurt that much because you're made of fur and stuffing."

"Well, dat's not true cos it hurt me quite a lot, especially when der arrow was pulled out, and I don't like dat YOU WERE TRYING TO KILL ME!"

"Okay. I suppose that might be quite personal."

Wrooph was increasingly incredulous.

"Don't you have any remorse for what you did? You're saying you've set out to kill Teddy three times! Doesn't that seem *wrong* to you?"

"I try to rise above questions of right and wrong."

"Horse poo! You're just trying to find a way to do wrong things and not feel bad about it. Would you like it if someone tried to kill *you* three times?"

"No, but here I am trying to make sure that doesn't happen, so I don't have to think about it."

"So you don't have *any* conscience about killing people?"

"Conscience? What's that!" laughed Pale.

"Woof! You are a *vile*. Perhaps it's easier killing from a distance with a crossbow; perhaps you don't have to see the face of your victim when you do it, but you've admitted killing a red Moccasin, whatever that is, and none of the things he might have done with his life will ever happen now. That's got to mean *some*thing to you?"

"Well, I think his days were numbered anyway."

"What do you mean?" asked Wrooph.

"Well, since it's increasingly unlikely that I can safely return to my master, I may as well tell you. Maybe telling you will help Teddy, and convince you that I am not a threat to you now. The Moccasins are being controlled. It's really very simple. So that little piece of red footwear would have had an 'accident' soon anyway. He was a threat."

"That's not the point; *you* killed him. *You* were the one who ended his life."

Pale didn't say anything. He just turned his head slightly away and reflected on Wrooph's words for a moment, and then turned back.

"You're making me feel uncomfortable. I want to you stop."

"No. I will not stop. I don't *care* if you're a bit uncomfortable, you need to hear these things. I know what it's like to lose someone and to be left behind when they've died. It feels like the worst thing in the whole world, and you're telling me you do that sort of thing to others all the time because 'right' and 'wrong' mean nothing? Well, it's wrong! *You're* wrong. WOOF! WOOF!"

Teddy edged up to Wrooph and stood side-by-side with him, comforting him with a simple touch of his paw on Wrooph's back. He continued the conversation because Wrooph could not.

"I ffink you are beginnin' to see what he means. I'm not very clever, actchually, and I ffink *I* understand him!"

"Well, I admit I have occasionally dwelled on what I do, but I consider it a weakness that eventually needs to be removed by discipline; not something to embrace. I deliberately *don't* think about the effects of my work. Perhaps that's something I have to do to be able do my job?"

"Perhaps you could get a new job?" asked Teddy naively.

"I ..." Pale began, but couldn't think of a response that properly countered Teddy's simple suggestion.

Pale looked annoyed; again he was feeling things that he didn't want to feel, so he turned away to remain detached.

After a moment Teddy had an idea.

"I want to find der Darkgate. Could *you* help me to find der Darkgate? *Dat* would be a new job for you."

"How do you know about The Darkgate?"

"I don't ffink dat matters, but could you be nice, and show me dat you're a friend, and help me instead?"

"Well, of course I *could*, if I *wanted* to. You might even argue that I *should* to protect myself. You've met Mole? He was working for us, and he has agents everywhere, and they always assume the worst, and I expect they've been listening to us talking just now."

Teddy and Wrooph looked around and sniffed.

"I can't smell anyone. I *think* it's safe."

Pale continued. "They're *clever*, you know. Anyway, I'm not a monster; I don't kill because I enjoy it. I do it because living or dying, right and wrong, are all equally meaningless, and I'm just making my way through life in the simplest way possible — but what you're asking of me is far more dangerous that you realise."

"Well, maybee it is, but *maybees* we need to do it anyways because I needs to find out what is happening. Can you tell us more about what is happening in Moccas? Can you take me to der Darkgate? Dat would be helpful and it would mean sumffin to my friends. Do you wants to help me?"

"Well, I don't know any more about the details of the Moccas operation, I was only there for one day to kill you, um, but The Darkgate, er, of course, um ..." flailed Pale, finding himself sinking into conflicting thoughts, threats on all sides, and disturbing feelings. Then he smiled a sly, crafty smile. Wrooph burst Pale's idea before it could take flight.

"Pale, stop thinking like that! You *will* take Teddy to The Darkgate, and I *will* come along too, to make sure you *don't* kill him on the way, like you're thinking of doing."

"My goodness! The thought had never crossed my mind," lied Pale, with a smile.

"Uh-oh. Ffank you Wrooph. I didn't ffink about dat. Are you really going to come too?"

"Hey, wait!" said Pale. "I haven't said I'll help you yet!"

"But you will, because otherwise I will deliver you to my master; I mean it."

"Damn. That again."

"And yes, Teddy," continued Wrooph, "I will come with you; this seems to be connected to Roffee's death."

There was little Pale could do, for now at least. He reluctantly agreed to take them to The Darkgate. All concerned knew that Pale would double-cross them at the first opportunity, but Teddy and Wrooph had to try. So they escorted Pale to the farm yard and introduced him to Naystraw and Gwen. Wrooph asked Teddy to tie Pale's bobbly arms behind his back with the ropes that were still outside Gwen's pen, and Naystraw had an idea.

"Iiiiy could taaake you aaall if you can hoooook me uuup to the children's caaaart?"

"Yes! Good idea," said Wrooph. "I think Teddy might be able to do that for us."

The farmer had made a small trailer for his children so Naystraw could pull them around the yard and the nearby fields while the farmer led Naystraw. It was roughly the right size for Teddy, Wrooph and Pale. The only problem was hooking it to the back of Naystraw's saddle. None of them were tall enough to reach and only Teddy had something approximating thumbs. They soon worked out how to do it: Teddy tied a piece of rope to the trailer's chain and Wrooph helped push Teddy up onto the saddle with his nose. Teddy pulled on the rope, and kept pulling until he had lifted the chain up to where he could grab it with his paws. He then hooked it over the question mark hook that the farmer had added to the saddle. Naystraw gently took up the slack and tried pulling the trailer.

"It works!" said Wrooph. "Now we have a chance of getting there and back before the farmer wakes up. If we're really going to do this then we need to do it quickly. What do you think?"

Teddy nodded and looked at Naystraw. He nodded too.

"This is a bad idea," cautioned Gwen.

"I have to find out what had happened to me at der Darkgate," said Teddy. "And I ffink we might find out about der Roffee too?"

Wrooph nodded.

So Teddy, Wrooph and a rather unwilling Pale climbed into the trailer, and soon Naystraw was clip-clopping out of the yard, and down the drive as quietly as a horse can.

::

Ten minutes later, Naystraw was happily cantering along the road at quite a pace. Occasionally cars would overtake them, but it was still well before dawn so they couldn't see much. Given Pale's appearance they all considered that a good thing.

Pale was clinically honest about things.

"You realise that I will have to make a choice? Will I listen to you and work with you? Or should I double-cross you at the first available chance, and hope that nobody saw or heard me telling you those things I said back there? I'm not sure yet."

"Nice. You're a murderer, but a murderer who tells his victims that he's thinking of killing them!"

"Well, I said it's nothing personal, it's just my job. If it *is* my job any more."

"What's der Darkgate den?" asked Teddy, cutting across the talk of murder.

"Oh, you don't know! When you mentioned it, I thought you

knew what it was! Oh this is classic! We're on our way to The *Darkgate*, of all things, and you have no idea what it is!"

"What is it doh?" asked Teddy, not understanding the joke.

Pale debated out loud with himself whether to give away more information.

"Right. This is how I see it. If I truly join you then I should tell you all that I know, so you will trust me. Of course, I could still double-cross you and kill you, or I could wait and hand you over because you would certainly die before they found out what I've told you. Hm, so I suppose either way, I can tell you."

"Just get on with it," grumbled Wrooph impatiently.

"Well, there are two types of answer to 'what is The Darkgate'. The first is that it's a pile of dark stones vaguely in the shape of cone. It doesn't look anything like a gate at all, and I don't know why it's called a gate. The second is that it seems to be the source of The Yorebear's power. When he touches it, it glows gold and he gets stronger. Its power allows him to fire 'forced light', as he calls it, at people — and then they die."

Pale stopped talking. Neither Teddy nor Wrooph knew what to say next. Teddy finally broke the silence.

"What's a yorebear?"

"*The* Yorebear," corrected Pale. "You really don't know much do you? He's the one who doesn't want you to go to Llandegley, and I'm the one who's taking you there! Oh what a fun day this is turning out to be!"

"But is he a bear? What is he?"

"Well, he doesn't look much like an ordinary bear, he's more like a human and he wears clothes, though he's got a bit of a snout like you, Teddy, and his clothes don't look like human clothes, they're simply skins and rags of material. Also he's very hairy. Much more than a human. I mean *really* hairy.

"I've never heard of The Yorebear before," said Wrooph, suspiciously. "How do we know you're not making this up?"

"Okay. Have you ever heard of the human King Arthur?"
Wrooph nodded; Teddy looked blank.

"He was a yorebear. 'Arthur' means 'bear man' in Old Welsh,
which was the language of all the Britons at that time, and there
were several yorebears back then, and many goblins ..."

For a moment Pale's normal cold, intellectual look was
replaced by a deep sadness.

"... but that was a long time ago. Those days are gone and
there's no way of returning to them. Now there's just one Yorebear;
the worst one. We simply do what we can to get through life."

Wrooph and Teddy looked at each other. Many questions
arose, even in Teddy's fluffy brain. How old was Pale? Was he
remembering these things? He seemed to know a lot about those
days; still, he seemed to know a lot about everything. However, if
Pale was living out his days, centuries away from the day of his
birth then the mystery of the feeling-less, disconnected Pale would
begin to make sense.

"How old are you Pale?" asked Teddy.

"Ah. That's an interesting question. In one way I'm very old
but then again I'm not much older than most old humans."

"What does *that* mean?" grouched Wrooph.

"It will make more sense when we get to The Darkgate."

A car overtook them just as they passed under a street light in
a small village and the passenger was horrified to see Pale.

"I get that a lot," said Pale. "We should probably get off the
road as fast as we can. The human police might be on their way
soon and we probably don't want that."

"For once, I agree with you Pale," said Wrooph. "Naystraw! We
need to get off the main road as quickly as we can."

"Weeeeee're neaaaaarly there nowww. Shaaaalll I keeeeep
going forrr a couple of miiiinits?"

Wrooph looked at Pale; they both agreed.

"Okay! Keep going Naystraw, but quickly!" Wrooph shouted.

Naystraw was right. Two minutes later they passed the sign for Llandegley and Pale directed them toward The Darkgate, down a narrow lane.

The sky was glowing from the East and it wouldn't be long before the sun rose from behind one of the hills; they had to do this quickly if they were to get back to Gaufron before the farmer woke up.

Naystraw trotted down the lane until he ran out of track at a turning space, which was completely surrounded by rusty metal railings except for the lane down which they had come. A path headed off from the turning area towards some trees, but it was gated. Pale pointed to it.

"You have to go down that path and round behind that wood there. You'll find The Darkgate at the end of the path," instructed Pale, looking very nervous.

"No, Pale. You're coming too," corrected Wrooph.

"You're *joking*! Do you have any idea what The Yorebear would *do* to me if he sees me leading you to The Darkgate? I mean it's The *Darkgate* for goodness sake!"

"You're coming, or I'll get Naystraw here to *kick* you over the gate and then I'll pull you there with my teeth."

Pale resisted as best he could but eventually he had to yield, appearing truly distressed for the first time since they met.

"Okay, okay," he said, nervously clearing his throat and swallowing hard. "But please cut me free? I have got to take my crossbow. Believe me, we will need it."

"And then you'll shoot us, or at least poor Teddy here," said Wrooph flatly.

"No. I *won't*. I mean I don't expect you to believe me, but after a rough start this is one of the best nights I've had in many years. It would be nice to continue, if you'll let me?"

"You're right," agreed Wrooph. "I don't believe you; Teddy keeps the crossbow."

"Damn you, you stubborn dog! You have *got* to let me use it if we need it! Please!"

"No. Uh-uh. No way. Teddy will have to use it."

"Um, I don't ffink my paws can do der clicky ffingy to let the arrow go," said Teddy.

"Grrr," said Wrooph. "Well, you should at least hold it until it's needed Teddy. I don't trust Pale."

"Okay den."

However, Wrooph agreed that Teddy should try to loosen Pale's ropes.

"Oh, that's no problem," said Pale, who simply shook his hands a few times behind his back. Teddy's knot fell apart immediately and the rope dropped to the ground. Pale smiled. Teddy looked crestfallen. Wrooph sighed.

Getting over the gate was not too difficult for any of them, although it took Teddy longer than the other two.

"We must hurry," said Wrooph. "It's getting light; my master will be awake soon."

"It's not your *master* that you should be concerned about, but you're right, we need to hurry."

So Teddy and Pale jogged down the path towards the trees and Wrooph pattered along beside them. Pale was terrified.

"This is my home," he whispered. "This is where I slept for hundreds of years until The Yorebear woke me and the others."

"Others?" queried Teddy and Wrooph at the same time.

"Yes, I tried to tell you this would be very dangerous."

"How did you go to sleepies for so long? Dat's a long time even for a teddy!" said Teddy, surprisingly jolly given the air of certain doom that had descended upon Pale.

"I haven't got time to tell you now; we're nearly there."

As he finished his words, dark stones became visible at the end of the curve of the path, behind the trees. As they jogged further on it was clearly a rough cone of stones, crafted by someone, or something, and not at all accidental.

"Please, *please* can I have my crossbow now? I really need it *right now*."

"No," said Wrooph firmly, stopping Teddy from giving it too him, but it was too late.

"PALE!" came a shout from the out of the wood. "WHAT ARE YOU DOING BRINGING *HIM* HERE?"

"I'M SORRY THEY MADE ME! THEY REALLY DID! YOU KNOW ME," shouted a quivering Pale, who proceeded to run next to Teddy to use him as a shield as best he could. Unfortunately Teddy wasn't tall enough and, since they were still running, he kept bobbing in front and behind Teddy.

"YES, I *DO* KNOW YOU PALE. YOU ARE A WORM. YOU WOULD TELL ANYONE ANYTHING, IF THEY THREATENED YOU."

The shape of a horse slowly emerged from the wood with a man on its back. To begin with he looked like any large, well-built man, then it became obvious he was not. He was covered in hair. The backs of his 'hands' were hairy; almost his whole face, apart from his snout-like nose, was covered in brown hair, and his shoeless feet were also completely concealed by what seemed to be like thick muddy fur. This was the Yorebear, and he was exactly as Pale had described.

"Well," panted Wrooph as he ran. "At least we know Pale wasn't lying.

The Yorebear was not alone. Following behind were a horde of other creatures, at least thirty of them, all equally as unusual as Pale. Some appeared to be oddly coloured dwarves; others were twisted and black and hard to make out in the dim, dawn light; a few looked like small humans that had been horribly damaged at some point in the distant past, and some were like mutated animals and humans with the wrong number of legs and arms.

They slowly advanced on the running trio.

"Get behind The Darkgate!" hissed Pale. "Quickly!"

Neither Teddy nor Wrooph commented, they just ran for The Darkgate.

Suddenly The Darkgate began to change colour. At first the dark stones seemed to change to a brownish black, then to brown.

"Oh no!" cried Pale. "He's going to use its power. Run faster!"

By now the stones were nearly orange, and then a bolt of light blazed between Pale and Teddy missing both of them by a few centimetres. Wrooph had made it behind The Darkgate by now, and turned, and was willing them forward.

"No! He's going to kill us!" shouted Pale.

"YES, I CERTAINLY AM, PALE!" bellowed The Yorebear.

Teddy and Pale were very close to The Darkgate now, but not close enough. The Yorebear fired again, from the palm of his right hand; this time hitting the ground on which they were running. Both Teddy and Pale were erupted into the air, surrounded by a mass of dirt and burnt grass. They landed and rolled for a moment before coming to rest only a few metres from The Darkgate.

The Yorebear raised his hand to fire again.

Teddy grabbed Pale's hand but it was hard for his paw to get a grip because of its slippery lumpiness. However, it was enough to get Pale to his feet, and Teddy continued running. Only Wrooph saw The Yorebear's third bolt blast into Pale, and by the time Teddy had reached The Darkgate all that was left of Pale was a smoking pair of rabbit skin shoes in the grass.

"Pale!" said Teddy. "He's dead!"

"And it'll be us next unless we can get to Naystraw," said Wrooph, nervously. "But how?"

Teddy, shocked and terrified, fell back against The Darkgate. It immediately made a hum and Teddy felt an exhilarating rush of power enter him. It felt good, intoxicating, hot, and at the same moment they heard a cold scream from The Yorebear, a thud, and the murmuring of a concerned horde.

"What was *that*?" asked Wrooph.

"I don't know," answered Teddy.

"You look ... stronger, somehow," said Wrooph. "And what was that noise from The Yorebear?"

Teddy peeped around The Darkgate. The Yorebear was lying on the ground, motionless and those near him were trying to prop him up and revive him. However, others further away from him were looking straight at Teddy and they called out.

"Get him! He did this!"

Teddy darted back behind The Darkgate.

"We have to go now I ffink, or day'll get us, Wrooph"

"Yep. Well, it's been nice knowing you, Teddy. You ready?"

Teddy nodded.

"Let's go."

They ran as hard and as fast as a dog and a Teddy possibly can. Not surprisingly, Wrooph was soon far in front of Teddy, a quarter of the way down the path. He realised that he was in danger of deserting his friend, so he stopped and turned around. The band of misfits were getting closer and closer to Teddy. It would only be a matter of seconds before they were upon him.

"Teddy!" he called out, hopelessly.

Teddy turned to face his impending doom and was reminded of the crocodiles a few months ago, but there would be no cars to save him this time. He stopped running, turned and shouted.

"Noooooo! I wants you to STOP! I don't LIKE IT!" and he put out his hand paws in front of him, like two stop signs. Immediately raw power shot out of his paws and annihilated the two creatures that were nearest to him, the power passed through their bodies and immediately killed two more behind them.

Wrooph couldn't believe what he'd seen. Teddy was amazed and horrified in equal measure. Then he turned back and sprinted towards Naystraw.

The horde of creatures were stunned, but it didn't take long for them to decide they still needed to pursue Teddy, only this time they ran while bent low in the grass, presenting as small a target as possible to Teddy.

Due to their awkward running, Teddy was now able to maintain the distance between himself and the vicious-looking creatures behind him, and there was a good chance that he would make it to Naystraw. Teddy was three quarters of the way there when Wrooph reached Naystraw's cart and jumped straight into it. At this, some of the braver members of the horde realised that they would have to risk their safety if they were going to catch Teddy. They stopped crouching and rushed towards Teddy.

"Teddy! They're gaining on you! Run faster!"

Teddy didn't answer, but his face was set with worry.

"You have to fire again Teddy!" called Wrooph.

Teddy didn't want to kill anyone else, but he knew those behind him had no such qualms. He had an idea. He stopped, turned and pointed both of his hand paws at the ground, in front of the horde.

"AAAARRRRRRRRRRRRGGGGGHHH!" he shouted, and the light fired out from his paws and detonated the ground in front of the murderous group thundering behind him. As before, dirt and grass erupted from the ground but Teddy didn't wait to see what happened, he twisted back and continued scurrying towards Naystraw's cart.

"Naystraw! Start moving!" called Teddy.

"He's right Naystraw" agreed Wrooph, as he willed Teddy to go faster from the back of the cart.

So Naystraw, who had turned the cart in preparation for their escape, started to pull, slowly at first. Teddy bounded up the gate faster than he'd ever climbed a gate before, and the next second he jumped from the top towards the cart. As soon as his paws had left the gate, Wrooph could tell Teddy wasn't going to make it. Teddy was flying towards him but his outstretched paws would be a good few centimetres short of the back of the cart, so Wrooph did the only thing he could do: he stretched out of the back of the cart, with his jaws wide open, and bit down on Teddy's paw in mid-air. Teddy's feet paws hit the ground and he bumped along the stony track for a few seconds, but eventually Wrooph pulled him into the cart.

"Ow. Dat hurt," smiled a very grateful Teddy, now lying on the floor of the cart.

By now most the creatures had picked themselves up from where Teddy's last shot had felled them, and run around the crater he had made. Some were clambering over the fence, others were vainly throwing stones, but they were powerless and many looked oddly dazed and tired. But Teddy, Wrooph and Naystraw were safely on their way.

In the distance a crossbow lay on the ground, its bolt still ready to fire.

::

It was about seven o'clock by the time they reached the farm. Luckily for them all, the farmer had gone on an errand in the far field so when they arrived there was no one else in the yard, apart from Gwen who was looking through her gate nervously for any sign of their return. They had time to tell her what had happened, and tried to make sense of what they had witnessed.

They decided that Teddy should try to fire light from his paws again, to see if whatever power he had gained was still working. Wrooph and Teddy carefully left the yard to find a spot to blast, without being too obvious, and Teddy raised his paws to fire. His paws glowed for a second or two but no light came out.

"Perhaps you need to be angry? Try thinking about something that makes you cross," suggested Wrooph.

"Pale, dead" said Teddy, and he tried again.

This time light came out of his paws and the grass burned where it landed, but that was all.

"I ffink it's run out of power," he said.

"I think you're right," agreed Wrooph. Then he saw something. "What's that under the bush there?"

Teddy poddled over. It was a bag made of rabbit skins. Inside was a small book, some food wrapped in rags, and a glass-stoppered bottle with water in it.

Teddy opened the little book and studied the writing on the first page. It took him a while to read it, but slowly he read it aloud to Wrooph.

"This book is owned by Archus, The Pale Goblin. If you find it then I am dead. If I'm dead, you probably killed me. If you killed me, you are better than me. If you are better than me, this information is rightfully yours."

"Even in death, Pale's annoying logical," said Wrooph dryly, but his eyes were sad.

Teddy thumbed through the pages of the book. There were maps and drawings. Lists and dates and diary entries. All written carefully and cleanly.

"Oh no. I ffink dis is a list of doze Pale has killed."

"-Remembering Gotar the goat. Died by the hand of Pale. Remembered forever by Pale.

-Remembering a rabbit of Llandegley. Died by the hand of Pale. Remembered forever by Pale."

Teddy slowly scanned down the list.

"Oh no," said Teddy putting his paw to his mouth. "Dis is horrible. Listen to dis."

"-Remembering Maaroon the sheep. Died by the hand of Pale. Remembered forever by Pale."

"He killed Maaroon! He killed her!"

Wrooph walked over to Teddy and nudged him with his nose.

"It's alright. Pale's dead now, he can't hurt anyone else. Maybe you should look at another page?"

Teddy thumbed through the book looking for things that might be interesting. Near the end, he found something.

"Cltha-llandegley!" he exclaimed, "he's written bout it!" and he read what he had found.

"This place of Llandegley, the place in which I have lived and slept for so long, is a special place, an old place. Even today, the local sheep remember that something is different about it. What they don't remember is why it is special but I, Pale, remember.

The Black Yorebear oppressed the people of Llandegley, and I decided to stop him. At night, the villagers took the stones from The Darkgate that had been built into their homes, from nine places throughout the parish, as described in the notebook that I had stolen, and I already had the tenth. Before we could strike, the nine families were killed; I only survived by lying and willingly joining the sleepers, and although there was success, and The Yorebear and the rest of us slept for a time, we are now awake again and they are no more. There is no point in trying any more, there is no good or bad, there is only power and those who use it, and those of us who survive do so by using power over others."

Wrooph was blinking more than usual and his eyes looked a little watery. Neither of them knew what to say. So Wrooph changed the subject.

"Um. Not that I want you to go, Teddy, but we need to organise your trip home. You need to get in that Landrover trailer over there before my master returns."

Teddy folded up Pale's things and put them back in the bag.

::

Wrooph's master was going to Aberystwyth to buy fence posts and fencing, and was then going to help herd sheep for his cousin who had caught a bad cold. He was looking forward to it because he'd have an evening out in town, then he'd stay at his cousin's overnight. He was much too preoccupied to notice a dirty teddy hiding behind a bag of feed in his trailer.

When it was time to go, Wrooph jumped up into the trailer and the farmer pulled out of the yard. It was luxurious to be driven around while chatting with Wrooph. Teddy could enjoy the hedges and fields and hills as they flowed by at a sensible pace, and they could chat without threat. Although Wrooph could be a little sharp, Teddy could understand why. Teddy had seen things that helped him understand something of Wrooph's loss and hurt.

As they chatted they discovered that Wrooph was vaguely related to Gruff, and Wrooph had also heard tales of Ramgar, and was very interested to hear Teddy's stories. Sheep were clearly no longer Wrooph's favourite animals, but he was wise enough to understand the importance of Ramgar. Teddy also told him not to believe any rumours he heard about his relationship with The Dolls, nor his involvement with the Moccasins, but Wrooph didn't know about either of those things, so Teddy spent the next ten miles giving him the details.

After Teddy had finished telling his tale, they both became quiet, mulling over the things that had happened. Teddy missed Agnes and wished he could get a message to The Dolls somehow, in case they were worried, but maybe Rufus was more important to them these days.

Teddy looked at Wrooph and gently envied how he belonged somewhere, to someone who cared, and remembered how Gruff had had a similar relationship with his master. Teddy needed something like that too, but what if Simon and Joanne were so cross with him that they threw him out? Teddy kept trying to imagine how they might react when he got home. He needed to belong again, he was out of place, lonely and missing something. He had felt awful after his encounter with Lady Teddy, but to be rejected by his old family would be even worse because Simon and Joanne *had* loved him, and now maybe they'd hate him, then he'd be ... Teddy stopped himself. He'd seen good and bad on his journey, and he had to believe that Simon and Joanne were good.

The Landrover and trailer wound its way slowly up to the pass at Eisteddfa Guirig, and then they began their descent towards Aberystwyth.

Many people dash through the landscape trying to get to their destination, but most farmers drive slowly, because they know there is no rush in life. Nevertheless, even at this mellow speed, it would not be that long before Teddy had to get out. Wrooph had offered to bark wildly, as if there were something very wrong. He hoped that this would make the farmer stop to see what was going on. Teddy was concerned that Wrooph would get into trouble, but he brushed it off. The farmer would shout at him, and be a bit annoyed but nothing would come of it. He'd make it up to the farmer later on, when he had to round up the sheep.

For a while they gazed out of the trailer at the view. Teddy decided that he liked dogs; they made good travelling companions.

By now they were very close to Teddy's home. They drove over the top of a pass and down into the valley, and Teddy saw his his old house.

"Dare it is," said Teddy, pointing.

True to his word, Wrooph started woofing like a mad thing. After a while, the farmer shouted out of the window for him to stop, but Wrooph got firmer and more persistent, barking again and again. The farmer shouted louder and shook his fist out the window, and kept on driving. This continued all the way down into the valley. It didn't look like he was going to stop. Teddy was getting desperate. He had to do something right now. So he stood up and waved at the farmer in his rear-view mirror and shouted 'STOP' to him. It was an obvious thing to do really.

::

In the lounge of Simon and Joanne's house, Simon and Bertie were sitting side-by-side, while Simon read aloud a book called, "Can you Find My Chicken?" Suddenly there was a violent, dangerous sound, the sound of rubber tyres squealing on the road because some desperate emergency required far more than the vehicle's brakes could ever hope to deliver. The sound was coming right at them. Then an instant-and-an-age later, the air was filled to bursting with the crunching sound of metal ploughing into brick at speed, and the breeze-block front yard wall erupted upwards into spinning chunks, flying high into the air. At the same time, the wall's powerful destruction slowed the Landrover spectacularly quickly, ending in it becoming a stationary, extremely damaged Landrover, mere centimetres from the front porch.

Bits of blocks rained down from the sky, bouncing on the metal of the Landrover, hammering big dents, and making querying sounds on the bonnet.

Finally, everything was lying quietly on the ground.

Simon gulped, stood up rigid, then rushed for the front door. The key wouldn't turn quickly enough. The door opened, and he was out into the porch, then through the outer doors, outside. He turned to see a man in the driving seat of his truck rubbing his head, but not apparently badly injured. Then Simon heard a familiar voice from the back of the truck.

"Uh-oh. Dat was *NOT* supposed to happen"

"T ... Te .... Teddy?" stammered Simon.

"Simon! It's really good to see you!" said Teddy happily. Then he stopped, as the fear returned. "Ummm. Simon, do you, um, still like me?"

Simon wasn't sure whether to burst into tears of happiness, or be extremely angry, so he did both.

"You, stupid, stupid teddy! Where have you been? We love you, and you disappeared! We were so worried!"

The farmer in the Landrover looked at Simon like his head was an enormous talking turnip, and he couldn't quite understand how. Simon noticed and stopped talking, and then remembered that the man might be hurt, so he ran over to check on him.

"You okay?" he asked.

"Yeah," affirmed the dazed driver, as manfully, but soon revised his opinion. "Well, no. Not at all, ooh, headache, and ..." and he silently touched other places on his body that hurt.

"Okay, I'll phone the hospital" said Simon, and he ran back into the house and told them the details of what had just happened outside his house.

In the meantime Teddy climbed down and also checked on the farmer, who found it hard to speak English to Teddy because it was too much of an effort when he was hurt, the pain now taking hold, and because he was trying to talk to a talking teddy bear. So all Teddy did was pat the man on the head, which made him wince, and then Teddy also went inside, carrying Pale's belongings. The farmer was now very confused.

An ambulance soon arrived. The farmer had three badly bruised ribs, and a bruised shoulder, whiplash and somehow he'd managed to break a bone in his hand. He also had concussion and, since he was miles from home, the doctors decided that he should spend the night in the hospital, which was not the night out that he had intended.

Luckily, Wrooph was fine. He'd bumped nastily into the trailer wall, but it was flat and smooth, so it wasn't too bad for him. The only sign it had happened at all was a slightly dog-shaped dent in the front of the trailer. Even the trailer itself was in surprisingly good condition because the Landrover had ploughed a path for the trailer to follow. It hadn't even jack-knifed. Wrooph explained that his place was with his master, so he stayed outside while they waited for the ambulance.

Teddy was very relieved that no one was permanently damaged, this was all his fault. He had wanted to apologise to the farmer again but Simon had convinced him that it wouldn't be a good idea. While waiting for the ambulance, Simon had asked the farmer why he had braked so hard. The farmer had been embarrassed and said he'd 'seen something' in his rear-view mirror, and left it at that.

Soon the ambulance left and took the farmer to Bronglais hospital, and his cousin arrived, looking ill and concerned, to look after Wrooph, and an hour or so later a recovery crew came to take the Landrover and trailer to the garage. After that Teddy and Simon were alone.

Simon re-introduced Teddy to baby Bertie and explained to Teddy that Joanne was at a conference in Birmingham. When at last Bertie was asleep in bed, Simon and Teddy were able to sit down and talk properly.

Teddy told him why he'd left, and the story of his travels. He felt it unexpectedly easy to recount how Lady Teddy had dismissed him without a second thought, but pangs of friendship and love when he recounted the wonderful help of the dwarves, and The Dolls. He also told Simon how he was worried for The Dolls, and the dwarves, and the Moccasins and sheep, and he confessed how worried he'd been about coming home.

"But you're glad to be here now?" asked Simon.

"Yes, I am. Dis is where I belong. Dis is my home. But, I miss my ffrends, and I worry."

"After all the things you've seen, all the individuals that you've met? I'm not at all surprised."

"Dat's right! Dat's it exactly."

"That's okay. What else could you do? They're part of your life now. They're part of who you *are* now. Maybe we can help you though? Maybe Teddy and Simon and Joanne can work *together* to help your friends. Would you like that?"

Teddy welled up with emotion. He wasn't alone any more. He had help. Big grown-up human help, and they would help him sort it all out.

"I'll tell you something though," said Simon.

"What?"

"You really, really need a wash."

"Not in der washing machine!"

"No," laughed Simon. "Not in the washing machine, but you could probably do with a shallow bath, if you could manage that?"

"I ffink," said Teddy. "Dat's a good idea. It's better dan a stream."

::

Teddy spent an hour in the bath and enjoyed it more than he ever thought possible. It was warm, and he felt clean, and the smell of poo receded a lot. Simon dried him with towels and they went downstairs to sit and chat in front of the fire in the lounge.

The next morning Teddy poddled into Bertie's room, and said 'good morning' to him in his cot. Bertie, who was almost five months old now, loved it because five-month-old babies see amazing new things every day, like televisions and aunts, and new types of fruit, so playing with a walking, talking teddy was no different and baby Bertie was delighted.

Although Bertie occasionally tried to nibble Teddy, and got goo on him, Teddy didn't mind nearly as much as he used to. Better yet, there was no danger of poo or wee landing on him because Joanne and Simon had become rather more expert at putting Bertie in his nappies.

Bertie loved Teddy, and Teddy loved him back. He enjoyed helping Bertie to play with toys, to learn to sit up, and when Bertie needed to rest, Teddy didn't even mind being a makeshift pillow. Best of all, Bertie wasn't screaming anywhere near as much as he had done all those weeks ago because his kidney problem had righted itself.

Joanne came home two evenings after Teddy had returned and, like Simon had been, she was angry but relieved. She'd been prepared over the phone by Simon and that had taken some of the sting out of it. Then, when all Teddy's tales had sunk in, Simon and Joanne realised that they had been partly to blame for Teddy's unhappiness and they vowed never to let it happen again. And the day after Joanne got back, the whole family set off for Bredwardine to take Teddy to The Dolls. They parked in the pub car park opposite the bridge, and Teddy walked off to see The Dolls on his own. It was better that way because it would have been impossible for Joanne, Simon and baby Bertie to have rolled up the gravel drive without previously announcing their arrival to Mother.

The Dolls were overjoyed to see him, having been certain he was dead, and Teddy was given a phone number that allowed him to talk to Agnes, Rufus and the other Dolls whenever he wanted. He reported all the things he had seen and told them what had happened to him, and they agreed that he should phone every few days, and come to visit every two or three weeks. Odd things were still happening, though perhaps at a reduced rate. Certainly, the stories about Teddy were also circulating less aggressively now, but the lies were not completely gone and even affected the Dwarves, with local sheep being told that Dwarves had killed sheep at night. The Dolls initiated an information counter-attack, with the support of the Dwarves and Ramgar, and all three felt stronger and glad to be working together.

However, the biggest surprise for Teddy was Bertie's teddy, Gundy. She was much smaller than Teddy, about the size of a large doll, and very pretty. When Teddy had left, she was totally inanimate, but now that Bertie was hugging her, she was showing signs of Waking. Teddy talked to her every day, and looked after her when Bertie got a bit rough, and cleaned her if she got gooey. He always believed that she might be able to hear him. Then one day, as he was cleaning her up, she looked into his eyes and smiled at him, and Teddy realised that there was a real, warm lady teddy, lying in his arms.

Epilogue

In the months that followed, Teddy became very close to Gundy, as she Awoke. It was no surprise to anyone except Teddy when he finally realised that he utterly loved her. It was certainly a relief to Gundy who had adored Teddy from the moment she had first seen him.

The family continued to take Teddy to The Dolls. Each time he was there, he was happy to see how they were improving their loving relations with those in their daily lives, which in turn made them stronger. His relationship with Agnes was still warm, despite her now being officially partnered to Rufus but, since Teddy had Gundy in his life, it was only a little bit awkward.

After a few months, Teddy even introduced Gundy to Agnes and Rufus. Rufus had nudged Teddy and told him that Gundy was gorgeous, only to turn around and find Agnes tapping her foot at him with her hands on her hips.

The Dolls, Ramgar and the Dwarves frequently met up and sent messages to each other, trying to find a way to counter the lies about them all. Then one day they realised that the lies were under control. The killings had stopped too, but by then the Three Moccasins had become The One, just Black. Black himself had become seriously ill, muttering and flapping uncontrollably, aided now by three bright Red helpers who essentially administered the Moccasins of Moccas. A few months after that, the three Reds and Black had a meeting with The Dolls, Teddy and Rufus, and all of them agreed to help each other, and to share information, but from the Moccasins there was still no explanation for Black's mental state, or the deaths of the other four of The Five, they simply said that there were some things that they wouldn't discuss, but not to worry because all that was behind them now.

Relations with the dwarves were as strong as usual, with all the Dwarven camp aware of the true stories about Teddy. Since neither Ramgar nor The Dolls ever left their localities, The Dolls sent Rufus to meet Ramgar, and both enjoyed their meetings. Ramgar's influence, while damaged, was still strong enough that even the Dolls' local sheep were willing to talk to them. Things were going well and no one was sure why, but it seemed likely it was something to do with the fall of The Yorebear at The Darkgate.

However, Teddy still wished he knew what had happened after Pale had poisoned him. Who had saved him? How had they countered the poison? How had they put him on Naystraw, and was it to keep him safe?

::

Months ticked by and Bertie learned to crawl and walk, and then he started to talk. He loved playing and chattering with Teddy and Gundy, blissfully unaware of the things that had happened in Teddy's life.

A few weeks after Bertie turned two years old, Joanne found out she was pregnant again. Teddy decided that this time he would face the new baby's noise and goo with stoicism, and Gundy assured Teddy that they would deal with it together, and support Joanne and Simon and Bertie. "After all," she said, with a wink, "it's easier than walking to Clehonger."

Then one early summer's day, a letter arrived, with the words 'FOR THE BEAR:' on the outside. It hadn't come with the postman, it was posted through the door by hand. He opened it and in it was a single piece of paper, with just these words written in the middle:

MAE'R TRYDEDD HENARTH WEDI DEFFRO
THE THIRD YOREBEAR HAS AWOKEN

Cold fear filled him, like ice prickling out from the core of his stuffing to the tips of his fur — the writing seemed the same as the note he had found on Naystraw's saddle all those months ago. Somebody out there knew about The Yorebear, and they knew he had woken up. Or maybe it was a different yorebear? Either way whoever it was thought Teddy needed to know this news now. And they knew where Teddy lived.

Teddy wasn't sure whether the note was a warning, or a call to action, but something needed to be done. He climbed the stairs to show the note to Gundy.

www.ingramcontent.com/pod-product-compliance
Lightning Source LLC
Chambersburg PA
CBHW070853120626
46556CB00002B/972